Praise for Patrick
The

You'll surely be drawn in by the magnificent descriptions of the scenery that portrays this apocalyptic world to such an extent that it felt as though I was seeing it in front of me. Not to mention the detailed and quite creative gore that completely blew my mind toward my happy place, namely 'my-imaginative-horror-land.'

—www.pissedoffgeek.com

The story has one of the fastest-paced plots that I've ever read. Each time the characters found refuge, they were harried by a mass of zombies in the next paragraph. Exhilarating is a word I would use to describe this story.

Into The Dark was a very interesting story and a little addicting. I want to read more about this band of people and their struggles to elude the zombie threats around them. This is a story that is about more than just the zombies. It's a narrative about very flawed human beings.

—www.livingdeadmedia.com

This book is full of fast-paced action, emotion, and creativity all wrapped up into one exciting package. It's filled with good zombie-bashing action like all good zombie novels should be, but it also pulls at your heart strings and really makes you root for Jeff to pull through all his struggles, and there are a lot of them. It has a very good pace and never gets boring.

The second book of the Dark trilogy is even better than its predecessor in both content and pacing. It starts off with action and keeps you in the story until the very end.

—www.dollarbinhorror.com

Comes the Dark is nonstop action. It feels as if you are watching a movie that you can't get up to go to the bathroom because you might miss something. D'Orazio portrays the undead in the best light: hungry, vicious creatures with a destructive appetite.

With *Into the Dark*, D'Orazio grabs the reader and pulls them into this story with a large violent hook and you're stuck, but what does happen is you don't mind being stuck, actually you love it.

—Sonar4LandingDockReviews

Comes the Dark doesn't take awkward stabs at making big changes in the zombie formula. Instead it is an unflinching look into how the normal everyday man in Anytown, USA deals with the world getting eaten alive in front of him. The zombies are prominent monsters; staggering and howling for flesh whenever the characters stop for a breath or supplies. I enjoyed the mix of good character building and tense action as it seems often times zombie stories sacrifice one for the other.

—Horrornews.net

There is no lack of gore or violence in these two books. Lots of action—not heavy with philosophical conversations or rants. The only problem I had with the books is that they were over too damn quick. I can't wait for the third book, and I highly recommend this trilogy.

—www.zombiephiles.com

Comes The Dark was an exhilarating read that kept me going, and Patrick D'Orazio's apocalyptic world is a dismal wasteland that will remain etched in your mind.

With *Into The Dark*, the new band of characters that we are introduced to are well drawn. A very diverse group of survivors with very different personalities create a lot of the conflict in the story.

—www.buyzombie.com

Comes The Dark is a very "grab you by the seat of your pants and drag you through the mud" look at the life of a normal everyman during the aftermath of a zombie outbreak.

—www.doubleshotreviews.com

Comes The Dark is quite possibly the best zombie novel I've ever read.

—Matt J. Nord, Publisher, NorGus Press

What a spectacular relationship dynamic between the two central figures. Their interactions are realistic and very well done. And an excellent job is done establishing the personalities of not just the main characters, but also those brought in as supporting cast. D'Orazio takes his time letting you get to know these people, preventing them from just being names on a page. Each one gets established with a genuine identity. The two-dimensional, generic characters that tend to dot the zombie landscape are not a problem here.

With *Into The Dark*, once again, D'Orazio gives a clinic on creating characters that are more than the sum of their parts.
—Todd Brown, author of *Zomblog* and *Dead, The Ugly Beginning*

Comes the Dark is well written, relentless, fast-paced horror. Be ready for blood, carnage and a wild ride in this tale of the Zompocalypse!
—Stephen A. North, author of *Dead Tide* and *Dead Tide Rising*

A tense apocalyptic survival tale with a powerful heart at its center.
—David Dunwoody, author of *Empire* and *Unbound & Other Tales*

Comes the Dark by Patrick D'Orazio is a high-speed adrenaline ride through the madness and insanity of the zombie apocalypse. From beginning to end, you question your own sanity and strength through the eyes of the characters.
—Benjamin Rogers, author of *Faith & the Undead*

Zombie fans should find plenty to enjoy here. D'Orazio has created an intense, character-driven story that will have the reader turning the pages very quickly. An incredibly impressive debut novel.
—Tony Schaab, author and creator of TheGOREScore.com

Comes a brooding tale of zombies in a world gone wrong. Patrick D'Orazio brings us a big book of zombie gore and mayhem. This one should keep you up long past your bedtime.
—Timothy W. Long, author of *The Zombie Wilson Diaries*

BEYOND

—Patrick D'Orazio—

THE DARK

Book 3 of the Dark Trilogy

Beyond the Dark
By Patrick D'Orazio
Copyright 2011. All Rights reserved

ISBN10 -1461089158

ISBN13 –9781461089155

Edited by Michelle Linhart
Cover art by Philip R. Rogers
Interior formatting by Kody Boye

This book is a work of fiction. People, places, events and situation are the product of the author's imagination. Any resemblance to actual persons, living, dead or undead, or historical events, is purely coincidental.

I would like to dedicate this book, the final in the trilogy, to my sister, Denise. More specifically, I dedicate the existence of one of the characters in this trilogy, Megan, to her as well. Denise, like Megan, may have looked small and weak on the outside as the trials she suffered through took their toll, but her strength and determination were incredible and far greater than anyone else I have ever known, up until the very end. She touched countless lives and demonstrated what it truly means to be strong and caring. She will be remembered forever by everyone she knew.

We all love and miss you, Niecy.

APPRECIATION

Well, it's finished. This book marks the end of this trilogy and the end of a long and winding road for me. Along the way, I've made plenty of new friends and have appreciated the support of many people who have been with me far longer than the urge to get published has existed. I've thanked many of them in the past two books, but it is only fair to bring them all back for an encore. And since I may never have the opportunity to demonstrate my gratitude is such a public way again (though I hope I get the chance to write some more novels), I wanted to make an effort to explain why I am grateful to each of them. So bear with me as I ramble a bit.

Let's start at the beginning, which is always a fine place to start. More thanks than can ever be relayed through this meager medium go out to my wife and kids, for reasons both obvious and not so obvious. My wife, because she has shown more patience toward my writing efforts than I ever have had the right to expect, because she believes in me more than I do myself, and because she keeps me from falling into a dark abyss of self-loathing on more occasions than I care to admit. My children, because they inspire and motivate me to be a better man, a better dad, and to set a good example for them with all that I do.

My parents and sisters—the people who helped turn me into someone who could step out into the world bravely and confidently, but who also remind me on a regular basis where I come from and who I was long before all this writing stuff took hold of me.

Special mention goes to David Ravitch and Kevin Callahan, who helped me with much of the National Guard information that I used not only throughout this trilogy, but also in another short story I created that takes place in the same world. Their information was invaluable, and I must state that they get the credit for all details that are accurate. Any glitches are due to my own goofs because I didn't listen to them well enough or ask the right questions.

For the people who read either one or many of the early incarnations of this book and the others in the trilogy, I am grateful. You all somehow believed that this was going to happen and that I would be published, from the beginning of this journey onward. That alone is worth so much, but the fact that you continued to encourage me and give me feedback means more than you know. So to Steve Vonderhaar, Joe Roman, Amy LaRoche, John Boehm, Mike Olsson, and Rob Cima, thanks. Not all of you read everything, and some of you read more than I would have ever expected, but at one point or another, you all made a tremendous effort to be encouraging and supportive, and you believed in me, even when I doubted myself and my ability to create this story.

Then there are the folks I met over at the Library of the Living Dead forums who encouraged me after I started the arduous process of beating the manuscript into shape and retooling it for release. Folks like Stephen North, Tim Long, and Ellie Knapp. They were the ones who looked at the first few chapters I had written and offered suggestions, tweaks, etc. that helped continue the process of improving this beast.

After that, there were the people who helped me put the actual books together: the publisher, the formatter, the editor, and the artist. This group includes Mike West, a.k.a. Dr. Pus, Kody Boye, Michelle Linhart, and Philip Rogers. Thank you one and all.

There are those people who have been there more recently, over the past year or so, who have made the effort to help me promote my work and who have been supportive throughout the process of getting my name and the name of my books out there. They have offered help, helped "pimp" me and the trilogy on the Net and at conventions, provided editorial suggestions and other ideas to make it all better. Thank you one and all: Ben Rogers, Beth LaFond, David Dunwoody, Tony Schaab, Matt Nord, Lee Hartnup, Felicia Tiller, Stephanie Kincaid, and the entire gang over at the Library of the Living Dead.

And finally, there is you, the reader. Thank you for taking the time to read my little story. If you are reading this book, I hope that means that you have read the first two books and enjoyed them enough to give this one a shot. I am truly humbled that there are a few folks out there who actually like what I have written, and that keeps me motivated to keep writing and keep getting better at this stuff. I am grateful to you, one and all.

Patrick D'Orazio
July 2006-January 2011

INTRODUCTION

As Patrick D'Orazio's Publisher, it is my distinct pleasure to write the introduction to "Beyond the Dark", the third part of "The Dark Trilogy". The book is a wonder to behold. Why you may ask? The answer is simple ... "Comes the Dark" and "Into the Dark" are two of the finest horror novels I have ever read or published. They are constantly at the top of our "Best Seller" list and continue to be snatched up by the book reading public. Do I expect this for "Beyond the Dark"? You bet your Aunt Bessie I do!

Reading the three books you can see how Patrick has honed his craft. His use of words is sharp. His descriptions are second to none. His "got ya's" are always well placed. Patrick's muse is firing on all eight cylinders.

So you, Dear Reader, are in for one of the great treats in the zombie genre of books. Patrick has written another winner. If you haven't read the first two books, please do that first. Then pick up this wonderful addition to "The Dark Trilogy". You don't want to miss any of the screams that will come from your inner soul.

Undead love to all,

Doc
Publisher
Library of the Living Dead Press

Prologue

The end came for the human race with a whimper, not a bang. The mysterious virus engulfed the world in a matter of days. Everyone infected seemed to die ... and then rise again. Governments collapsed, armies disappeared, and entire civilizations turned to dust as the human race tore itself to pieces.

Jeff Blaine managed to survive the first waves of destruction as he hid behind the barricaded doors of his suburban home with his wife and children. But it wasn't long before the hell that was outside broke through his defenses and destroyed all that he knew and loved.

Now, with his family gone and his life in ruins, the only things left for him were bitter pain and anger. So, as he ventured out into the desolation, he had no better plan than to destroy as many of the monsters that stole his life away before they destroyed him as well.

But it didn't take long for Jeff to discover other survivors. Megan, who had also been hiding out in her own house, was afraid of the world, but gained strength from realizing that she was not alone. George was a man who clung to the hope that his wife and two daughters were still waiting for him at home. And Jason, a sullen twelve year old, found it hard to trust anyone anymore.

Together, the survivors begrudgingly agreed that they would help George find a car to get back home and then the other three would try to find a place out in the countryside, far away from the hordes of plague victims that wanted to destroy them. But all they found were more of the dead as well as other survivors even more desperate than they were—desperate enough to steal and kill to get what they needed.

It didn't take too long before Jeff and the others were captured by a group of survivors hiding out in an encampment buried in the woods. Their makeshift fortress consisted of several RVs parked in a circle to shelter them from the dangers of the outside world as they quietly hid away from the undead that surrounded them. Their leader, a charismatic man named

Michael, spoke passionately of the human race's need to survive and how he believed his tiny settlement contained the seeds that would help civilization be reborn. He maintained strict control over the camp, refusing to let anyone leave the safety of his sanctuary, except on a dangerous mission to collect food and other necessities from a nearby town.

When the trip ended with the death of one expedition member and another bitten and infected with the virus, the survivors returned to the camp with a horde of the undead following in their wake. Michael and a few other members blamed Jeff for the failed mission, causing a heated division among the members of the camp. The group was forced to fight for their lives, first attempting to make a stand against the undead and then realizing their only hope was to flee the camp in one of the RVs, despite the long odds against their survival.

I had a dream, which was not all a dream.
The bright sun was extinguish'd, and the stars
Did wander darkling in the eternal space,
Rayless, and pathless, and the icy earth
Swung blind and blackening in the moonless air;
Morn came, and went and came, and brought no
day,
And men forgot their passions in the dread
Of this desolation; and all hearts
Were chill'd into a selfish prayer for light ...
From "Darkness" by Lord Byron

Chapter 1

The survivor's lungs were on fire as he jogged down the street. It felt like there wasn't enough oxygen in the air, and stopping to rest for long wasn't an option. Glancing to his left, he saw the shattered picture window of a Chinese restaurant. The temptation to step inside faded as long shadows danced off the buffet table and booths that had been knocked over inside. There was no movement out on the street, and the area appeared to be abandoned, but there was no telling who or what might be roaming around inside the building.

The man felt a twinge in his side and slowed to a stop. Leaning against the exterior of the building, he bent his knees until they popped, and tried to catch his breath. All he needed was a few seconds and he would be good to go again.

Looking up, the sweat-soaked renegade stared through a display window of the store adjacent to the restaurant. Nothing was left inside except a thick layer of dust. The restaurant and the store shared the ground floor of a block-long two-story brick building with two other businesses. The desperate man wondered where there might be stairs leading to the second floor at the back of the store. What was up there? Apartments, perhaps? A view from a window with a higher vantage point might help him find the person whom he sought ... but that was far too risky a proposition and would take too much time. He needed to stay on the hunt.

Another burst of gunfire shattered the silence, and his head snapped up. The noise echoed and bounced off the different structures in the surrounding area, but it was clear from which direction it had come. Several loud moans followed, but the volume was nothing like it had been back at the camp. It was a smaller cluster of ghouls making this racket. The rotting horde had broken up and spread out as the survivors fled the accident in different directions. But even a smaller mass of the monstrosities was dangerous and impossible to manage for even a well-armed group.

With a grunt, the solitary traveler got moving again. The gunfire had stopped, though the moans continued. That was how things had gone for a while now: big chunks of silence broken by gunshots and distant moans.

The only time it had been different was when he had heard the screams.

They had not been cries of terror. Instead, there had been pain in them ... agony, to be more specific. A sound such as was heard when the undead tore into their victims, clawing at their skin and ripping the meat from their bones. It was a sound with which the survivor was quite familiar. Thankfully, when he heard the screams this time, they didn't last long. It wasn't a sound to which you never grew accustomed, no matter how many times you heard it.

One of them is dead, he thought. At least one was, maybe more. The gunfire had disappeared, but that had happened before. They might all be dead, but he had to be sure. There was no way he could stop tracking them until he knew for certain.

Jeff wiped greasy sweat off his brow and looked at the back of his hand. There was no blood this time. The thin cut above his eye had stopped bleeding. The sweat he'd smeared into the wound stung, but he barely noticed. Gripping the baseball bat, he forced his tired legs to keep him moving toward the sounds he heard up ahead.

Chapter 2

The crowd of decrepit figures had spread out enough so that the RV could pull away from the other Winnebagos without bogging down. Michael drove out into the open, smashing through bodies that burst like putrescent balloons beneath the windshield or bounced off the bumper.

It was one giant right turn at first. The Winnebago Destination was a thirty-nine-foot Class A motor home with a huge diesel engine, and weighed around fifteen tons. It rode smoothly over the rough surface as Michael spun the wheel, holding it steady. He swept around the other vehicles, going clockwise, and sideswiped several trees as he dodged a large glut of rotters. There was a screech of protest from outside as tree limbs dug into the RV's silvery paint. Several bodies were tossed into the trees and pulped as they stood where wood and metal met. Michael overcompensated in response to the dying protest of the limbs by nearly steering into Lydia's RV, but recovered in time to straighten out. The entire time, his foot remained planted on the gas pedal. To stop was to die. It would give the ghouls enough time to clump up in front of them, clogging their route to freedom. The diesel engine roared as they plowed through bystanders in their way.

The noise outside was deafening. Any vocal cord that had not stiffened or decayed vibrated and thrummed with excitement. The sounds permeated every square inch of the RV, drowning out the screams of children and weeping adults alike. Michael increased his speed slightly as they slalomed through the open space with trees on one side and abandoned motor homes on the other. He plowed through the parade of bodies like they were bowling pins. Hugging the curve, he watched as more and more ghouls were crushed beneath the wheels. The shiny paint job was now crusted over with organic matter that splattered the RV like a Jackson Pollock painting. Michael's head pounded as his eyes darted back and forth, desperate to avoid any major impediments that might make him crack up.

The passengers sitting in the cramped confines of the bedroom in the back of the Winnebago stared through the windows, trying to snatch details of what was going on outside. Despite their fears, they couldn't help but look as they sped away from the place that had been their home. Seeing the other RVs from the outside, with all the blood and decay dripping down their walls like biohazard graffiti, made it hard to comprehend how those metal sentinels had kept them safe for so long.

Michael yelled for everyone to hold tight, snapping them out of the daydreams and nightmares they were all having. He twisted the wheel to the left, sending Megan sliding to the floor as Lydia clung to the children. Jeff grabbed a hold of Megan's arm and hoisted her back up on the bed. Everyone else gripped whatever stationary object they could find.

Jeff's van was the marker for which Michael had been watching. He had parked it east of their exit point, and it was a beacon amongst the swarm of bodies telling him where to make his turn. When he saw it pop into view, he knew it was time to switch directions.

He steered through the trees toward the field that lay beyond. Thankfully, the crowd had spread out enough to give him all the room he needed. There were still a lot of bodies to plow through, but not enough to hold the fifteen-ton vehicle back. The driver breathed a sigh of relief as he looked down the wooded tunnel that would take them to the outside world.

Michael knew the trip might only last a few minutes if the broken bodies got jammed in the wheel wells or the axle got clogged up as he rolled over them. Far too many military vehicles, even tanks, had gotten their wheels and tracks snagged with shattered flesh and bone. Only speed and surprise could conquer these bastards when they were in huge numbers. Speed, surprise, and a hell of a lot of luck.

As the mammoth machine forced its way through the narrow route between the trees, Ben, George, and Jeff moved forward in the RV until they were grouped around the small dinette table. They pulled back a shade and looked out, their eyes wide. The bloated and broken bodies kept coming, whizzing by the window. Many were knocked back as they blindly moved into the path of the Winnebago. But for every one taken out, two or more took its place.

The jumble of screams and inquiries about what was going on from the back slowed as they broke out into the open. Sadie and Nathan were still crying, inconsolable in Lydia's arms, but some of the adults clapped and cheered. To Jeff, it felt as if they had burst free from an infected womb, a nightmare threatening to imprison them forever.

The brief celebration died as everyone saw the field ahead.

"Sweet mother of God," was all George could say as they watched the huge packs of migrating bodies outside their window. He looked at Jeff and Ben, and neither could add anything to what he had said.

On the field to the north were even more plague victims than Jeff had seen back in Gallatin. They were pressing in from all directions, their agitation increasing as they saw the moving feast coming toward them. The ghouls traveled in clumps and clots like gangrenous scabs scattered across the earth's surface. They pushed and jostled one another, jockeying for position. Jeff blinked and looked at Michael as he attempted to navigate through the crowd. He avoided all the impenetrable knots and clusters while blasting through smaller groups that were more easily scattered. Up ahead, closer to the road, the crowd was thinner. The infected were spread out to almost nothing on the asphalt.

"Which way are we going?" Jeff yelled to Michael as he stood up and inched his way toward the front of the vehicle.

"Just sit back down and leave Michael alone!"

Jeff looked at Frank, who was seated in the swivel chair across from the driver. The one door on the motor home was directly behind his seat. Frank had a white-knuckled grip on the armrests as he swung around to face Jeff. Although he was angry, Jeff could detect a hint of fear in his voice. The hillbilly's face looked pale and had the consistency of cottage cheese.

"Look, I'll sit down, just tell me where you're taking us," Jeff said, raising his voice in an effort to cut off Frank. "I can tell the others ... maybe calm them down a bit, if you just let me know where we're going."

Jeff forced himself to sound meek as Frank and Cindy, who was sitting directly behind Michael, stared at him. Getting even this close to them was elevating his blood pressure, but he knew he had to play it cool.

"We're heading east, through Manchester and out into the country." Michael dodged another glut of stiffs before turning to glance at Jeff. "Does that meet with your approval?" The words came out in a sneer, the hatred coming off the driver in waves. Michael turned back to face the road, the steering wheel dancing in his hands.

Jeff felt naked as Cindy continued to glare at him, a nasty smile on her face. He wished he had his baseball bat, but it was in the back with Megan.

Fighting to retain his balance as the RV hit another bump, Jeff mulled over what Michael had said. They were driving into Manchester, which was insanity. Groaning inwardly, he knew what had to be said, but was already regretting the words before they left his lips.

"Going through town? Pardon my French, but are you fucking nuts? Do you see the same shit I do outside these windows? How many more of these crazed mother fuckers will we have to plow through if we go through town?"

Cindy bounced to her feet, the look in her eyes feral as she stalked toward Jeff. Her tattoos and raggedy mismatched hair gave her a wild, animalistic look. Her hands were tensed at her sides, claws at the ready.

Jeff stumbled back, but managed to stay on his feet. His eyes never left Cindy's as he waited for the attack. She had no weapon, but looked prepared to scratch his eyes out. He thought he heard her hiss.

"Cindy, sit the fuck down." Michael's voice was harsh, a nervous master ordering his pit bull to heel. "Jeff, I suggest you back off before Cindy shreds you to pieces."

Jeff's eyes darted over to Michael, but quickly returned to Cindy. He saw no change in her demeanor, nothing that would indicate she had even heard her boyfriend's command. Then it happened. If he had blinked, he would have missed the transition. Her eyes steadied, and she relaxed. Though an evil glint remained, she looked human once again. She continued to stare at Jeff for a few more seconds, then licked her lips and moved over to Michael. It was clear that both the driver and his guardian bitch had dismissed him.

Jeff backed up past the table where Ben and George sat and headed back to the RV's bedroom while Cindy continued to stare at him with ferocious hatred. When a wall was between him and the evil bitch, he was able to relax and give Megan an uneven smile, but wasn't able to breathe normally again until he collapsed next to her and Jason on the bed.

Chapter 3

This hadn't been the plan.

They were going to make it through Manchester, no problem. Just a few turns of the wheel and they would be past the pisshole town and out where there wasn't any population to give them more grief. All they had to do was dodge a few stiffs on the town's streets and they would be golden.

But they shouldn't have been out here at all. They should still be back at the camp, turning back the dead up on the walls, or better yet, sitting quietly with those ghoulish bastards none the wiser that they were there in the first place.

Of course, that was before that prick Jeff had screwed everything up.

Michael felt better about things once they got past the field. They were going to be okay. He felt it in his bones. Jeff was still bitching, insinuating himself in every decision made, but Cindy had put him in his place. Even with the tension that strummed on every one of his nerve endings, Michael felt an almost primitive pleasure at seeing Cindy unleashed. Jeff might have enough backbone to snipe at a man with an automatic weapon, but he had no interest in taking on Cindy in full bitch mode. Once she flicked out the claws, the best a guy could do was to avoid pissing himself.

They hit the asphalt of the street, and the vibrations that had been rattling the RV stopped. Michael's eyes swept the road, and he knew they would be all right. There were plenty of meat sacks milling around, but not enough to do any real damage to the beast he was driving. The ones on the road were even more clueless than the ones they'd left behind. They didn't seem to be sure what to make of the big vehicle; they were too busy stumbling around like some crappy imitation of the Keystone Cops. Michael's eye twitched as another loosely stitched rag doll disintegrated against the grill. Watching another one of them obliterated was only a minor pleasure by now, but the knowledge that he had put another pathetic bastard out of his misery still gave him a bit of a rush.

His black leather boot pressed down on the gas pedal as they sped past the car trap he and Ben had created. It was a nifty little setup. Too bad they had netted such a worthless bunch of losers with it. Michael gripped the steering wheel a bit tighter and clenched his jaw muscles until they ached. Rage whipped through him like a poisonous wind, and he pressed his foot down even harder, watching the speedometer inch up. Jeff's presence felt like a blood-sucking tick pulsating in his ear.

Soon.

That one word dampened the anger, took the edge off of it. They would be done with this stinking place, and then he would be done with Jeff for good. Once they got past the town, he could clean house.

Michael swerved to avoid a loose configuration of limbs and teeth waggling at him, excited and energized to see flesh behind the wide glass bubble of the windshield. One of the slugs pointed at him, and for a moment, he felt like a menu selection at some posh restaurant. He resisted the urge to run it down, straightening the wheel as the RV rolled past. He could not let his anger get the best of him. The distractions outside were nothing compared to the pains in the ass in the back of the RV.

Soon.

Chapter 4

The crash happened quickly.

Even if Frank had noticed the pileup in the middle of the street and warned Michael, they were going too fast to stop. As it was, Michael only saw the mess in the street at the last second and spun the wheel hard to the right as he slammed on the brakes. They hit the curb going forty miles per hour, and everything shifted as the rear of the Winnebago started to slide, the wheels on the right side of the beast going airborne.

They landed on their left side, the ground rising up to shatter the windows. After that, the sound of screeching metal running along the asphalt drowned out everything else.

When they stopped sliding, Michael felt nothing, but soon discovered several large chunks of treated window glass sticking out of his cheek and hands. There had been a huge *whump* when they made contact with the road, then he heard a sound like a thousand fingernails assaulting a chalkboard. The sound persisted, echoing inside his head as he lay strapped in the captain's chair behind the steering wheel. Thoughts flew through his head as he gathered his wits: What had happened? Was he dead?

Hearing a groan nearby, Michael looked up to see Frank dangling above him, his seatbelt holding him in place. He was conscious, but in a daze, his eyes trying to focus as he twisted and turned in his seat.

Thank God that fat bastard snapped on his seatbelt before the crash, or he probably would have crushed me beneath his blubbery ass.

Dismissing Frank for the moment, Michael's eyes wandered toward the windshield as he tried to puzzle out what had happened. It had cracked, but hadn't shattered. Glass had exploded upward as the left side of the RV made contact with the road, but that was underneath him. He had been wearing his seatbelt as well, which had prevented him from getting cut to ribbons as they slid along the asphalt.

Over the ringing in Michael's ears, he made out faint moans and several sharp cries of pain from the back of the motor home. He ignored the sounds as he twisted his head in an effort to see behind him.

"Cindy?"

Shifting his weight, Michael contorted his body, but still couldn't look backwards. He reached down to the seatbelt snap. It wouldn't pop with his weight pressing on it, so he put his left arm against the doorframe and braced his leg. He was careful to avoid more slivers of glass as he lifted his body off the strap holding him up. There was a clicking sound, and he was free. As Michael got his feet underneath him, he could hear glass grinding beneath his boots. He twisted until he was in a crouched position, standing on the left wall of the RV and looking toward the back of the vehicle.

What a total cluster fuck. Michael could hear more screams from the back now and almost called out for the others. He stopped short as he looked at Cindy. Her entire left side was bloodied where glass and the impact with the asphalt had wounded her. She had not been wearing her seatbelt and had gone flying into the wall, skimming across several jagged shards of glass as she did so. Despite her new horror-show look, she was already standing and didn't look all that dazed.

Michael shifted his eyes up to Frank as he heard him groan. The slack-jawed look on his face wasn't much different than his usual expression, but it was clear he was still groggy from the accident. His groaning continued as he shifted in an effort to free himself from his elevated prison.

"Don't undo your seatbelt, you idiot. You'll fall on top of me." Frank stopped squirming in his chair near the new roof and watched as Michael took out his knife. "I'll cut you down. Just don't land on your head. Brace yourself."

As he sawed at the belt, the ringing in Michael's ears abated. Now, in addition to the cries of panic and pain inside the RV, he could hear other noises coming from outside.

The infected were heading their way.

As he cut through the tough, fibrous material of the seatbelt, Michael could almost smell the fear on his sweaty underling. Frank was pushing up against his armrest, and Michael wondered how long it could hold his massive weight. At least Frank's effort was giving him enough room to slide the knife back and forth. Michael managed to cut through it in a few seconds, and after the final slice, he moved back toward Cindy, ignoring an imploring hand as it reached down from Frank's precarious perch to request help getting down.

"Well, how the fuck do we get out of here?" Cindy growled.

Michael stiffened as he got a closer look at his girlfriend. Her arms were crossed, and there was a vicious snarl on her face. She was bleeding from a thousand tiny cuts on her face and arms, and bits of glass were lodged in most of her wounds. In the half-light sneaking in through the windows surrounding them, she looked more like a ghoul than one of the living.

When Michael heard a thud behind him a moment later, he almost jumped out of his skin before realizing it was Frank.

"Damn it! I lost the gun!"

Michael looked back at the other man, who was scanning the RV's new floor for the missing .357 Magnum that had fallen out of his pants. It was the excuse he needed to look away from the horror that was Cindy's face.

Michael gripped the strap attached to the M16. It had stayed in place through the accident, unlike everything else. As he looked at the jumble of boxes and other stuff strewn out behind them, Michael frowned. They hadn't just lost the handgun. Many of the bags they had carried on board had burst open, and an assortment of clothing, canned goods, and other necessities was mixed together like some sort of strange potluck.

He sighed. "Leave it. Leave it all. We don't have the time to mess with this."

Frank looked stricken, but Michael ignored him. They were going to have to leave the other weapons behind as well. The rifles and shotgun were buried in the pile of crap on the floor with everything else. He motioned toward the front of the RV.

"Let's knock out the windshield."

When the bloody hand touched his shoulder, Michael almost screamed. He bit down hard on his tongue instead, gagging as Cindy spun him around. He could taste coppery blood in his mouth as he looked at her.

"What about the others?"

Michael stared into his girlfriend's eyes, doing his best to ignore her gore-peppered skin. Taking a steadying breath, he looked at the back of the RV.

The others were still trying to sort themselves out in the bedroom, and he heard a voice asking if everyone was okay. They were still in a haze back there. There weren't any seatbelts in the back of the RV, so chances were they had all been tossed around quite a bit, and there was a good chance at least one of them was dead. Wasting time trying to sift through the mess back in the bedroom in an effort to save the others was a surefire way to get them all killed.

Plus they all want you dead. The thought hit Michael like a punch in the gut. He wanted to deny the cold logic of the assessment, but he knew it was true. Even the look on Lydia's face after he'd killed Ray betrayed the fact that she'd lost all faith in him as a leader. Each and every one of them would betray him the first chance they got.

"Fuck 'em. Let's get the hell out of here."

Frank looked happy with the decision. His darting eyes made it clear he was ready to get out of the RV and make a run for it. Cindy looked somewhat more reticent about the idea of abandoning the others, but Michael knew it had nothing to do with any affection she might be harboring for them.

Michael pushed Frank aside and braced himself. Aiming his right foot at the crack in the windshield, he shot his boot out in a powerful kick, which landed with a thud against the tempered glass. Instead of the satisfying crunch of glass, he felt something pop inside his ankle. He resisted the urge to cry out as pain knifed through his foot and charged up his leg. Gripping the chair, the injured man pinched his eyes shut as he raised his foot, afraid to put it back down.

"Nice try, hot shot. Why don't you just use the butt of your rifle on it instead?"

Michael tried to ignore Cindy's snide tone as he stared at the windshield. His effort had created a few more spider webs, but the glass was still in place. Beads of sweat formed on his forehead as he tried to keep his breathing calm.

Tensing, he put his foot back on the floor. Although his ankle hurt like hell, he was certain he hadn't broken anything. Doing a reasonable balancing act, he slid the rifle off his back. Cindy was right about using it on the glass, though Michael hated to admit it. Careful to keep most of his weight on his left foot, he slammed the butt of the weapon into the glass. The pain was incredible as the blows vibrated his arms before the windshield gave way. When the glass finally collapsed, Michael pushed aside the remaining stalagmites and stalactites and limped outside.

Frank was glued to his ass, anxious to be free of the dungeon the motor home had become. Cindy hesitated, staring toward the back of the RV, watching and listening as the other passengers collected themselves.

"Quit fucking around, Cindy! We've gotta get moving!"

Cindy ignored Frank's nervous command as she squinted, looking back into the gloom of the motor home one last time. The sun was bright, but not shining directly behind her, and it floated through the windows and danced on the wreckage, swirls of dust moving lazily over everything.

The door near the back of the RV was opened. Two of the men had been outside the bedroom when the crash occurred, and one was already at the edge of the wall, leaning over it, trying to help those stuck in the back. The other still lay on the floor, unmoving.

She wasn't interested in either of them. Cindy stood on the tips of her toes, desperately trying to see inside the bedroom. She cursed silently when she got nothing better than a glimpse of frantic movement beyond the Good Samaritan at the doorway.

With a sigh of regret, the bloodied woman turned and climbed out of the shattered windshield. As she did, the man on the floor opened his eyes to watch her leave. When he was certain the punker girl was gone, he searched the debris surrounding him. He stopped when he found what he had spotted earlier and shoved the object into his pocket. He then stood up and turned to help the other man with the rest of the passengers.

Chapter 5

Michael led the way as the threesome moved away from the wreckage. It was easy to steer clear of the ghouls that were shambling toward the RV. The sounds of shouting and cries of pain from inside the vehicle were enough of a lure that none of the rotters seemed too interested in following the fleeing trio. Leading his small contingent down one of the nearby cross streets, he was able to gain some separation from the milling corpses.

His ankle was throbbing, but he discovered that if he was careful, he could put some weight on his foot and maintain a decent walking speed.

"You okay?"

Michael shot Frank an angry look.

"What?" Frank stepped back, out of Michael's range. "I just wanted to make sure you were all right." His voice sounded defensive and whiny as his eyes traveled from Michael's face to the M16 and then back down to the ground.

A grin nearly split Michael's face in half. Frank couldn't have made his desires any more obvious. The fat man was unarmed for the first time in forever, and it was not sitting well with him.

Michael dismissed Frank for the moment and studied Cindy, who kept looking back at the RV. He slowed his pace until he was walking next to her.

"Feeling a little guilty, my darling? Do you want to go back and help the poor little plebes?"

Cindy's head whipped around, her expression menacing. Michael continued to taunt her.

"You go right ahead, sugar britches. Go save those poor little lost lambs."

It was clear he had struck a nerve from the growing look of resentment on Cindy's face. She did want to go back to the RV, for whatever twisted reason. Michael moved in for the kill.

"Sorry, sweets, no time for more of your games. But I'll tell you what: if one of your pals back there happens to get up after that crowd of stiffs is done with them, feel free to turn around. Then you guys can have all the fun you want, okay?"

After watching Cindy glare at him with raw hatred for a few seconds, Michael grabbed her shoulder and pulled her close. His voice had been soft and taunting up to that point, his eyes sparkling with amusement. Now his face was dark and tight with anger, his words coming out in a hiss.

"Listen, Cindy, I'm done with your bullshit. We're not turning around to save those dumb fucks just so you can torture them some more. Just get that idea out of your thick goddamned skull so we can focus on more important things, like getting the hell out of here."

The sly smile that appeared on Cindy's face threw Michael off. Her hand slid around his neck until she was able to run her fingers through his dark brown hair. He did his best to ignore her ravaged face as she gently pulled his head toward her lips until they were close enough to graze his earlobe.

"I'm really sorry, baby," Cindy whispered in a husky voice. "But it looks like they're not the only ones that need saving."

She nibbled on his ear, gently tugging at first, but then Michael felt a sharp pain as she sank her teeth in, ripping away part of his earlobe.

"You stupid bitch!" Michael screamed as he gave Cindy a violent shove. Her laughter sent a spike of anger through him as she landed hard on the asphalt. Grabbing for his ear, he hissed in pain as his fingers met raw, torn flesh. Cindy continued to laugh hysterically as her boyfriend's blood dribbled down her chin. As the shock of what had just happened wore off, Michael limped toward his assailant, a homicidal look in his eyes.

"Michael ... MICHAEL!"

Michael cursed and turned to see what was so important that Frank was screaming at him.

There were two stiffs coming toward them.

Michael felt his skin grow cold, and the anger with Cindy evaporated as he stared at the ghouls.

One was small, withered, hunched over. The other stood tall and ramrod straight, its spine unaffected despite its having been dead for several weeks. They had crept out of a store nearby whose door was hanging wide open. They made a fine odd couple: one looked like a little old lady—stiff, brittle, and fighting a monumental case of arthritis, while the other looked like a young boy who had been cut down in the prime of his life. It looked like the younger of the two had a lazy eye, but Michael realized the socket had been traumatized and the eyeball was floating freely inside the creature's skull. Its other eye stayed focused on Michael. The old woman (or man or deformed child ... he really couldn't tell) let loose with an excited moan, and a thick pus-colored liquid spilled from its mouth.

"What, don't you find me fascinating anymore, darling?"

Michael ignored Cindy's mocking words as he slid the M16 off his shoulder. Gripping the weapon in both hands, he drove the butt of the rifle into the face of the taller ghoul. Not waiting to see the results of his handiwork, he winced and shifted his weight, hip-checking his geriatric opponent to the ground. Turning quickly despite his ankle, he saw that Stretch, as he had dubbed the taller stiff, was still vertical. The rotting creature had stumbled backwards from the blow to its nose, but hadn't fallen. Michael advanced and slammed his rifle into Stretch's head once again, ignoring the outstretched arms reaching for him. His blow connected with the boy's forehead, and there was a satisfying pop as the younger assailant crumpled to the ground, inert. Michael gritted his teeth at the throbbing pain in his ankle and looked over at the older fiend, who was having a hard time getting back up. Before he could make a move, Cindy advanced on the aged ghoul. As the brittle creature reached out to grab her, she raised her right leg and brought it down hard on the bridge of its nose. Black goo squirted from the new fissure in its skull as Cindy ground her heel into the thing's face. When its arms stopped twitching, Cindy stepped back to wipe her dripping shoe on the pavement.

Michael glared at Frank as his dumbfounded crony stared at the remains of the ghoul near Cindy's feet. "Feel free to jump in any time."

Frank looked confused, and his eyes grew wide. "I thought … I thought you were gonna shoot them."

"Idiot," Michael mumbled under his breath as he turned and began walking again. He slung the rifle over his shoulder as he gently touched his bleeding ear. He would deal with Cindy later, but his first priority was to find a working vehicle so they could get the hell out of Manchester.

A quick glance around confirmed that there were plenty of cars, but none looked drivable. Someone must have had some fun with fire as things got out of hand in the town. Several businesses had been torched, along with most of the cars lining the street. A few charred bodies inside some of the automobiles made Michael wonder if they had already been infected when the fires came or if they were just poor fools who'd gotten caught up in whatever riot had consumed the area.

It wasn't long before Michael's sense of urgency was spectacularly reinforced. As the trio continued moving down the street, a dark shadow blotted out the sun momentarily and a body landed nearby. It sounded like a bag of mushy potatoes as it splattered all over the pavement. Cindy had seen the shadows shift and yanked Michael back from the point of impact just in time. He stumbled back and yelped in pain as he put his weight down on his bad leg, but Frank's scream of terror drowned him out completely.

"Will you shut it? You're going to bring the whole town down on us if you keep up that crap!"

Frank's mouth slammed shut as he stared up at the two-story building from which the ghoul had jumped. When it appeared that no more bodies would be following the first off the rooftop, he gave Michael an apologetic look.

"I'm sorry, man, but this shit is really starting to freak me out," he moaned, his voice on edge as his eyes darted back and forth. "I wish I still had my shotgun. Damn, I miss my baby."

Michael was ready to lay into the whiny idiot when four figures stepped out of an alleyway to their left. The rotters were already on top of them—just a few steps away and closing fast.

The sound of rifle shots filled the air. Michael ripped off two three-round bursts and watched as four bodies fell to the ground, their spoiled brains dripping on the asphalt.

Cursing silently at the noise, Michael kept the rifle out as he limped down the street as fast as he could. He had just announced their presence to every stiff in town. Frank bounced along beside him, bumping up against the other man repeatedly, like a dog whose leash was too tight. As he did, he verbalized what Michael was thinking.

"We're fucked now, man! They're gonna keep coming at us!"

As if Frank's words had magical power, several moans echoed off the steel canyon of buildings surrounding them. Michael slowed, trying to get a fix on where the noise was coming from. Frank skidded to a halt as Michael gestured for silence. He swung the rifle in front of him in a wide arc, hoping to spy movement ahead.

"Cindy, do you see anything behind us?"

Michael knew how doggedly persistent the infected could be. They were able to track a normal person with uncanny ease. Chances were, in this small downtown section of Manchester, that the three of them were already surrounded. But if they could move a few blocks in any direction, they would be out of the cramped urban setting and have more room with which to work. The injured man could feel his ankle stiffening up and knew they were running out of time.

"Cindy?"

He looked back when there was no response. Frank did as well, and they scoured the landscape. Michael's blood began to boil.

"Where the hell did she go?" Frank asked, baffled.

Michael screwed his eyes shut and clutched the rifle to his chest. The temptation to yell for Cindy was strong, but he already knew where she had disappeared to and why. It would be pointless to call out to her. She would ignore him.

The crazy bitch had abandoned them.

"I should have killed you when I had the chance," was all he could mutter as he shook his head in disbelief.

Doing his best to blot his psychotic girlfriend from his mind, Michael tried to focus on more pressing concerns. The moans were getting closer.

"Oh shit."

Michael opened his eyes at the sound of Frank's fearful voice. He raised the M16 to his shoulder and stared at the shifting shapes out in front of them. There were six in all, the closest about half a block away. More moans were coming from behind but didn't sound as close.

Frank grabbed Michael's shoulder and pointed at another batch of ghouls coming from their left. They were everywhere. At present, the two men could only spot a few, but other rotting forms seemed to be boiling up from the earth like ants. Michael spun, not sure where to shoot first. Then something caught his eye. Tensing, he made a quick decision.

"This way."

Gesturing toward a side street that appeared clear of the undead, he limped in its direction. Frank moved forward, barreling ahead of his gimpy partner. There were more echoing cries of excitement as the stiffs closed on their position. Michael glanced back in time to see more coming, small groups merging to form a larger pack. He turned and kept limping down the road.

Frank glanced back, and Michael could see how tempted the cowardly bastard was to take off and leave him behind. But his beady eyes moved down to the M16 again, and the fat hick's expression changed. He slowed to give Michael a chance to catch up, not interested in being too far from the man with the weapon. Frank even smiled as he urged Michael forward, his loyalty on full display.

As they moved farther down the street, the moans grew louder.

Michael ripped off several shots in quick succession, switching the rifle to semiautomatic mode to preserve ammunition. He had only two thirty-round clips and had already burned through several rounds in the first one.

Only two of his targets went down as bullet holes appeared in the chests of several others. He cursed silently and scanned the buildings surrounding them in the hope of finding a safe haven. There were surprisingly few shattered windows or smashed-in doors, and there were only a couple of abandoned cars on the road, with no corpses lying out in the open. It felt like a massive and deadly contradiction: the bright sun casting its rays down on a relatively pleasant little street while two people raced to escape a couple of dozen ravenous cannibals trying to eat them.

"Michael, we need ... we need to get out of here! Please! Get us out of here. I can't handle this anymore ... please!"

Frank was losing it. If they didn't get somewhere safe fast, he was going to get them killed.

Gritting his teeth, the man with the rifle searched the area until he saw the perfect place for them to go. Michael knew it would solve all their problems. He raised his hand and pointed.

"Let's head that way. But you've got to help me, man, it's hard for me to walk anymore."

Frank glanced down the alleyway Michael had pointed out. He could see daylight peeking out from the opposite side. It was narrow, but not a dead end. Frank continued to quaver, but nodded in agreement.

Michael slung the rifle and lifted his arm. Frank slid underneath it and allowed the taller man to lean against him. They moved toward the alley at a brusque pace while a slow parade of rotters followed. Despite their awkwardness, the two men managed to increase the distance between them and their pursuers while closing in on the narrow opening between the two buildings. Michael looked back, satisfied at the distance between them and the nearest hunters. As they moved down the alley, he gripped Frank's shoulder and urged him to slow down. Frank anxiously obeyed.

"You know, Frank, I've been thinking."

Frank looked up at the man he had obeyed dutifully for over a month, his expression filled with hope. Michael was smart, and when he focused on a problem, he typically came up with a solution.

"You need a weapon. I think my knife will work," Michael said as he unsheathed the blade.

Frank frowned, disappointed. "Thanks, but no thanks. I'd rather have something I won't have to fight up close and personal with."

Michael shook his head. "I'm afraid I must insist."

When the knife entered Frank's belly, his expression didn't change. It was only when Michael drove the blade deeper that the bolt of pain hit and the heavyset man looked down to see the hilt protruding from his gut. Frank looked back up at Michael, confusion stamped on his face. He shook his head as if to reiterate that he really didn't want the knife.

Michael wriggled out from Frank's grasp and pulled the knife free. Without the other man to hold him up, Frank slumped to the ground, landing on his knees. His thick fingers covered the wound as he stared at the blood gushing out of it. As he toppled backwards, he screamed.

When Frank felt the hand on his leg, he shrank back toward the wall and stared at Michael, his eyes wide with fear. Only when he saw that his former friend was trying to say something did he stop screaming.

"... truly sorry. I really am."

"Wha-? Why ... Michael? Michael! What have you done to me?"

Michael shook his head and grimaced as he leaned in closer and clamped his fingers even more tightly around Frank's leg. The other man was too busy trying to hold his guts in to squirm out of the iron grip. Frank kept looking down as if he expected his organs to start spilling out of the hole in his belly, but so far there was only blood.

He started to cry, and Michael shushed him like a baby, raising a finger to his lips and shaking his head back and forth, a stern look on his face. Before Frank could blubber even more, Michael spoke again.

"I'm sorry, Frank. I really am. But you're just too damn weak." His fingers dug into Frank's calf, but the injured man didn't seem to notice. "I can't babysit you any longer."

Frank felt another sudden sharp pain, this time from his ankle. For a moment, the agony in his belly was forgotten as Michael's knife cut efficiently through his Achilles tendon.

Michael stood up, a grunt of pain escaping his lips as he balanced on his good leg. A look of grim satisfaction claimed the murderer's face as he stared at the mouth of the alley.

Frank howled as he tried to wrap his fingers around the sliced ankle, recoiling in pain the instant he touched the wound. Groaning heavily, the fat man tried to lever his body up the alley wall behind him, but only made it a few inches before slipping back to the ground, exhausted.

After a few moments, Frank's eyes refocused on Michael, who was still backing away. His limp was far less pronounced now.

"You were a good soldier, Frank. Weak, but a good soldier nonetheless. You should feel proud of what we accomplished together."

As Michael stared down at the bloody mess Frank had become, the hamstrung man lay motionless, his eyes dull as they stared back at the man who had betrayed him. His crying had stopped; perhaps he was going into shock

A small group of undead appeared at the entrance of the alley. They sniffed the air as they came, drawn forward by the rich coppery scent of Frank's blood. The one at the front of the pack raised its head and caught sight of Michael at the opposite end of the narrow passageway. For a moment, their eyes locked. Michael felt an icy finger sliding down his back, and he blinked. When his eyes opened, the dead man was focused on the fallen form of Frank, which was far closer. Michael watched for a couple more seconds, certain that something had passed between him and the ghoul. Whatever it was, it made him feel more discomfort than fear, as if the wretched creature somehow knew he had betrayed Frank, and had judged him for it.

Wiping the sweat from his brow, he turned, fleeing as quickly as his wounded ankle would allow. He had exaggerated his injury to fool Frank, but it still hurt mightily. After running the knife blade along his pants to get rid of Frank's blood, Michael sheathed the weapon at his wrist.

*

Frank watched as Michael's form diminished. He wasn't in shock, but his thoughts were getting fuzzy. The pain had been incredible at first, but there was a numbness creeping into his belly and ankle as more blood flowed away from his open wounds. That helped keep him from crying out in agony, which was good. Tears still blurred his vision, and he knew he had to figure out a way to get back on his feet. He had to drag his sorry ass down the alley and follow Michael before any of those flesh-craving lunatics found him. As his fingers dragged along the dirty concrete in an effort to gain purchase, he tried to blot those horrific bastards out of his mind.

I won't die. I can make it. If I can get back on my feet, I can limp along. The gut wound isn't so bad. I just need to get stitched up. Lydia will do it for me when I find her.

Frank's wet fingers slid into a mortared groove between two bricks on the wall, and he tried pulling himself up once again. When his fingers slipped and he fell back to the ground, a small whimper escaped his lips. *I'll get back to the others and they'll help me! They have to!* A small sound like a hiccup escaped his lips as he grinned.

"They'll take me back. They'll forgive me for abandoning them," he insisted aloud.

The only response he got was an excited moan from behind where he lay on the ground. Frank hiccupped again, laughter trying to force its way to the surface. He couldn't go any farther. He was stuck, and someone was coming for him. There was a small desire to turn and look, to see who it was. He wanted to believe it was Lydia. Dear, sweet old Lydia. She would comfort him, take care of his wounds like she took care of everyone else who'd been hurt. She wouldn't care that he had run off with Michael and left them behind to suffer and die. She was too much of a saint to hold a grudge.

The moans grew louder, and Frank finally understood. He wanted to ask God for forgiveness; he wanted to pray for some sort of redemption. But instead, he felt rage building inside as the sound grew louder. He could hear awkward footsteps sliding along the hard surface of the pavement. They were getting close. Only a few seconds left to live, and Frank knew he still had a choice. He could ask for forgiveness and hope for a charitable God to grant it, or he could continue to think about Michael. The unholy bastard had hamstrung him and hadn't just left him to die; he'd left him as bait.

There were more footsteps dragging closer. Too many to count. A whole army. That was when Frank made up his mind. He screamed again, the rage outweighing any terror he felt. It was not some high-pitched wail that escaped his lungs, but a single word repeated again and again for whoever remained in this wretched world to hear.

Even as the monsters tore into him, ripping his flesh and rending his bones, he screamed, howling his curse on blood-flecked lips until he could scream no more.

*

Michael had made it a block when Frank's first scream pierced the muggy air. He stopped and looked back at the gap between the two buildings he'd just escaped. There weren't any bodies tumbling out in pursuit.

The plan had worked. Frank's immobile form had been too much of a lure for the mob to pass up. As another scream burst forth from the alleyway, Michael knew his crony would keep the ghouls occupied for a while.

The screams grew higher in pitch and then cut off abruptly. Satisfied, Michael continued down the road. He made it a few more feet before Frank screamed out again.

"Miiiiichaaaaaaaeeeeeeel!"

Even as the dying man's ragged voice faltered, he continued to shout. Michael could not outdistance the sound, even as it turned into one long, final scream that never seemed to end.

He limped along as fast as he could, a small whimper escaping his lips as he realized what he had done.

Now he was truly alone.

Chapter 6

Ben frowned as he scanned the area. He had just stepped outside through the broken windshield to get an idea of how much trouble they were in. He and George had already hoisted Jeff over the back wall, and the two other men were dealing with the women and children still inside the bedroom.

They were in the center of Manchester's small downtown area, surrounded by shops and office buildings. Ben saw the pile of cars that Michael had been forced to dodge, which had sent them skidding into the curb. But it wasn't what he saw that bothered him; it was what he heard. The howls of the infected. Ben's eyes narrowed as he spotted the first of them on the street. As he surveyed the neighborhood, he saw more coming. There wasn't much time.

Moving with purpose, Ben went back inside the RV. George and Jeff had just lifted Teddy's unconscious body over the bedroom wall with Lydia's and Megan's help. Jason, who had a huge gash on his forehead, was straddling the barrier and assisting them as best he could.

Ben performed a rapid evaluation of the two men standing before him. George was the bigger and stronger of the two and looked like a linebacker who could probably plow through a pile of stiffs like they were nothing. Jeff was physically average and didn't strike Ben as the athletic type. He was just another soft suburbanite. Yet it was clear that there was more to Jeff than that. The end of the world had changed the man. That was apparent from the way he had stood up to Michael and stuck with Ray even when the boy had been as good as dead.

Making his decision, Ben stepped forward.

Grabbing Jeff by the arm, he pulled him out of earshot. After a few seconds of furtive whispering, Jeff nodded and scooped up the baseball bat lying at his feet. They made their way outside.

"Holy shit," was all Jeff could think to say as he saw the bodies pouring out of the buildings surrounding them.

"How long do we have?"

"A couple minutes at the most." Ben saw the fear on Jeff's face morph into grim determination and knew he had made the right choice.

"What do we do?"

"We need to distract them. All of them."

Jeff looked around again as he felt his skin grow cold. His teeth started to chatter, and he clenched his jaw to make them stop.

"We need to tell the others."

"You do it. I'm going to get started." Ben moved away, but turned back to say one last thing. "Don't take too long. Just tell them to get the hell out of here and find someplace to hole up. Whichever way they go, head in the opposite direction. I'll find them, wherever they go."

And he was off, whooping and hollering as he charged into a group of staggering forms, bowling them over. Jeff watched in amazement as Ben kept running, his wild movements and bellowing voice drawing attention from every cloudy eye in the area.

Jeff's heart pounded as he scrambled back inside the RV. He was relieved to see that everyone was out of the bedroom and George already had Teddy's unconscious form over his shoulder.

George gave him a questioning look, but Jeff ignored it as he faced Megan. As he closed the distance between them, she smiled. Her expression changed as she saw the look on his face.

"Take the kids and find someplace to hide."

The words hit Megan like a ton of bricks. Jeff grabbed her hands. "I'm going to try and lure away as many of those things as I can from."

Megan's eyes widened as she heard the sounds from the street. Everyone else was coming to the same dark revelation. The crash had been so traumatic that no one had the time to think about anything other than getting out of the smashed-up RV, until now.

"How many of them are there out there?" Lydia asked.

Jeff gave her a bleak look that told her everything she needed to know. She had Sadie in her arms, and Nathan and Joey clung to her, dazed and frightened as they stared at Jeff. Everyone could hear the howls and cries of rage building in volume as the undead that hadn't been distracted by Ben's antics drew closer to the RV.

Jeff dragged Megan forward, and the rest followed them until she set her feet and stopped him. "Wait a minute! You can't just leave us! This is insane."

Jeff turned to her, his eyes sad. "Ben's already left. He lured away as many as he could, but it's not enough. I have to do this."

Megan shook her head, tears flowing as she gripped Jeff's hands tighter. She tried tugging him back inside the RV, but he resisted and pulled her toward the broken windshield.

"Everyone outside now. Megan and I will be there in a couple of seconds."

Jeff gave a pleading look to George, who nodded solemnly. The older man herded the others outside, urging them forward as several sets of eyes remained on Megan and Jeff.

When they were gone, Jeff turned to Megan, who was already starting to mount a new protest. "Megan. Megan! Listen to me! If I don't do this, we'll all die. Do you understand me? But if I can get those bastards' attention, you'll have a fighting chance."

Jeff had a tight grip on her shoulders, and when Megan shook her head, he squeezed them until she stopped and stared up at him, her eyes wide with panic.

"You need to pull yourself together. Please! Do it for Jason and the children. Do it for me!"

Jeff's eyes burrowed into Megan, and she stared blankly in response. When he shook her roughly, she was able to blink and then nodded. Not giving her a chance to change her mind, Jeff yanked her outside. He pushed the stunned woman toward George, who wrapped his free arm around her before going back to staring at what was happening around them.

Ben had left a wake of bodies following his trail. Jeff could no longer see the big man, but it was obvious which street he had taken from the movements of the crowd. His heart sank as he saw the mass of bodies still surging toward the little group of survivors. Gripping his bat, he turned to the others.

Teddy had regained consciousness, and George and Jason were supporting his weight. He looked groggy and was the only person not staring at Jeff. Lydia had the children calmed down and seemed prepared for whatever she had to deal with. As Jeff's eyes moved toward Jason, he could tell the kid was putting on a brave face. It heartened Jeff as he looked back at George, who nodded in return. George understood what had to be done, that he was now the group's guardian. Jeff silently mouthed the words 'thank you,' and George gave him a sad smile. Finally, Jeff turned back to Megan. She looked miserable and angry and didn't speak as she glowered at him, her blue eyes icy.

"Get out of here," he said. He pointed at a street that appeared to be clear of shambling bodies. "Head down that way and try to find a place to hide out." Megan's expression softened as she realized he was serious about leaving them.

Jeff backed up. "I'm going to lead as many of them away as I can. Now move!" He started to jog in the opposite direction from the one in which he had pointed. Several staggering ghouls took notice and shifted away from the stationary group. Jeff's eyes narrowed, and his lips curled into a devious grin. Gripping the bat loosely, he picked up speed and took off running.

The last thing Megan and the others heard Jeff say as he

rushed the horde was, "Find someplace safe to hide! I'll find you! I swear to God I'll find you!"

Then he gave a loud war whoop as he swung his bat at a ghoul reaching out to grab him.

Chapter 7

George took the lead, ushering everyone away from the wreckage. They could smell the diesel fumes as they moved past the rear of the RV. The tank was cracked, and fuel flowed beneath their feet.

As they moved away from the intersection, George found a stout piece of wood that had been part of a doorframe, and Jason, following suit, found a slender piece of metal in a pile of crunched-up glass. Teddy, who was coming around, joined in and picked up a few chunks of pitted metal and rocks light enough to throw.

They moved north, up the road Jeff had recommended. He had lured most of the stray infected with him in the opposite direction, and their path was clear for the moment.

The small group was in the heart of town, with streets flowing in all directions. They were surrounded by buildings and storefronts for several blocks. As they moved, Lydia managed to keep the children calm and quiet by suggesting they make a game of it. Whoever could remain quiet the longest won. They were still terrified, but it served as a good enough distraction to keep them from crying out.

Megan suppressed her anger and disbelief at what Jeff had done as her survival instincts kicked in. She kept Nathan and Joey next to her, relieving a grateful Lydia of the burden of tending to them as George and the two older boys walked ahead, scouting in silence.

The survivors soon turned down a side street with several

free-standing buildings—offices, boutiques, and a couple of chain restaurants. The area appeared abandoned, and George suggested that they move a few more blocks away from the RV before picking a place to hide.

It was not long after George spoke that they heard the first shots. The sounds echoed off the buildings making it hard to pinpoint their source. Everyone froze. There was no movement nearby, so after a few moments, George urged everyone to get going again.

Megan had not thought much about Michael, Cindy, and Frank since the accident, but she guessed they were involved with the gunplay. She couldn't help feeling a twinge of guilty pleasure at whatever predicament they had gotten themselves into after they had so willingly abandoned her and the others. As a small grin of satisfaction found its way onto her face, she spied a ghoul staring at her.

A startled scream escaped Megan's lips as she watched the monster stumble out of the McDonald's they had just passed. The rotting figure's neck was broken, its head dangling from a bloated tube of flesh with split marks running down its length. It was like some over-ripened melon whose insides had burst free from the rind. A badly soiled uniform with a nametag pinned to it completed the picture. Megan could see that the teenager was named Jamie, and he was missing several fingers from the hand that reached out to her.

Nathan and Joey began to cry, tugging hard on Megan's hands, urging her to run. She remained frozen as she watched Jamie approach, fascinated by whatever dark magic was keeping him upright.

Jamie's skin had gone from gray to an almost brownish black. Though his neck was broken, his equilibrium seemed adequate enough to close the gap between him and Megan.

George rushed past, with Teddy and Jason close behind. Teddy let loose with one of his heavy chunks of metal, grazing Jamie in the shoulder. It did no visible damage, but served to knock the walking corpse off balance, and he stumbled before getting his uncoordinated feet back underneath him.

Jamie stepped out onto the street, stumbling between two crumpled cars with matching flat tires and shattered windows. As the infected boy moved beyond the wrecks, Megan noticed the way his sneakers flopped loosely around his ankles. The shoes had burst at the seams as Jamie's feet swelled with fluid. The canvas was like some sort of tent covering the huge blackened feet.

The thick piece of wood George wielded came crashing down. A spray of soupy gruel splashed up as Jamie's head popped free of his neck like a swollen tick. The boy's hands stayed elevated even as his body followed the trajectory of his detached head toward the ground. They finally flopped to his sides as the former McDonald's employee hit the asphalt.

"Is everyone okay?"

George wiped splatters of fluid off his face as he glanced around at everyone. They all seemed okay, but Megan had a dismal look on her face.

"I'm so sorry I screamed, George. I won't do it again, I promise," Megan said with remorse.

George shook his head. "Don't worry about it. Your scream warned me he was coming." He nodded toward Jamie's corpse. "We'll be fine as long as we keep moving."

Before Megan could say anything else, they heard more shots off in the distance. George strained his ears to ascertain from which direction the gunfire was coming, but he knew it was a pointless task.

Dismissing the sudden distraction, he patted Megan on the shoulder. "Come on, let's get going."

George moved back to the middle of the road, and the others followed suit as their eyes searched every doorway and window for more trouble.

Less than a minute later, two shapes separated from the shadows near a small shop and limped out into the open. Before George could react, the two teenagers leapt into action, darting in opposite directions. It was clear almost immediately that this tandem of rotters was even slower than normal due to a lack of muscle mass. They had been thoroughly mauled before turning, and only a few shreds of meat and tendon remained on their torsos. The boys lured the slow-moving creatures in separate directions, giving George the chance to take care of them individually with a few efficient swings of the heavy plank he carried.

Jason and Teddy were still high-fiving one another when Lydia spotted another group of stiffs coming out of a vacuum repair shop nearby. She was ready to yell to George, but he saw them only a split second after she did.

The leader was clad in motorcycle gear, and his left leg was chewed down to the bone. The remains of his torn chaps slapped against his leg as the monster limped toward Jason, his closest target. The biker reached for the boy and let out a froglike croak.

In his euphoria at his and Teddy's success, Jason didn't hear the low sound right away. It was only when the ghoul gave an excited squeal that he whirled around. Jason's eyes went wide as the biker grabbed his arm and leaned in to take a bite.

He screamed and tried to back up as the stiff lunged forward. The monster's teeth snapped on empty air, but it tightened its grip on the boy's elbow. Jason's scream changed from terror to pain as he felt something tear under his skin. The infected man pulled the twelve year old closer to his gaping maw, insensible of the boy's struggles to break free. The ghoul gurgled in anticipation.

George crashed into the biker, causing the rotter to release his grip on Jason's elbow and slam into the sidewalk. There was a snapping sound as several brittle bones broke in the monster's arm from the force of the blow. George kept rolling, avoiding the stiff's claws as he bowled into the other three creatures that had also come out of the vacuum repair shop.

Teddy rushed up and launched several chunks of metal and rocks at the bodies struggling to grab at George. He threw the missiles one by one as he steadily slid forward, focusing most of his effort on a particularly decrepit creature. George was throwing punches and landing kicks on the other two from where he lay on the ground, but the one on which Teddy had zeroed in had escaped the burly man's attention and was rising up to strike. As a sizeable stone bounced off the slug's head, it turned and hissed at Teddy. The boy's eyes were wild as he growled, "Come on!" and continued to taunt it.

Jason shot a glance toward the biker as he struggled to slide backward on his butt. It was clear his friends were too busy to help him, but the blinding pain in his elbow was making him dizzy. His movement was hampered as he cradled his injured arm protectively. Jason had no idea what was damaged; all he knew was that his arm felt as if it were in the steel grip of a vice. He could barely move it, but fear helped him ignore the jolts of pain as he inched away from the battle. The leather-clad ghoul's arm may have shattered, but unlike the twelve year old, the inhuman monster felt no pain. Its tongue licked the air in anticipation as it closed the distance between it and its prey.

Jason tensed, preparing to kick out at the looming figure as it got closer. The hand that had damaged his arm reached for him, and Jason bit down hard on his tongue, forcing himself not to scream. His eyes narrowed, and he waited for the right moment to strike.

There was a sudden blur of movement as Megan crashed into the biker. Jason could only gape in amazement as she lashed out with a thin, whip-like sliver of metal, jabbing it at the ghoul's eyes.

Before the biker could respond to the surprise assault, Megan was able to drive the broken car antenna she had picked up off the street through one of its eyes and deep into its brain. Wrenching it up and down, she screamed like a madwoman until the antenna broke off in her hand.

Rolling off the inert body, Megan popped up into a crouch as Jason watched in stunned silence. She scanned the area and saw that Teddy was in danger as well. He had whipped the last of his rocks at one of the ghouls that had been harassing George and was now preparing to go toe to toe with the rotter as it advanced on him.

Megan charged in like a halfback, plowing into the female ghoul's chest with the full force of her ninety-pound frame.

She landed on it with a heavy thud, and there was a whip-crack sound as its skull hit the pavement. Raising her hands to the leathery, tight skin of the monster's forehead, Megan slid her fingers into a tangle of hair. She drove the skull into the asphalt several times, her palm forcing the forehead forward even as her fingers yanked up on the scalp. She only stopped when a small spatter of liquid covered the pavement underneath the fractured skull.

As she rose, Megan felt the buzz of adrenaline dying inside, leaving her aching and exhausted. When she looked back to make sure the boys were okay, Megan's eyes widened. Teddy had already dragged Jason several yards away, and they were screaming for her and George to run. Turning to look past the vacuum shop, she understood why.

The screaming Megan had done as she attacked both ghouls endangering the boys had blasted her eardrums to the point where she could hear nothing else. Not Teddy's or Jason's warnings, or the screeching howls and moans as a second wave of infected rolled down the street toward them. All the noise the group had been making, all their screams and shouts to one another as their battle raged, had drawn a crowd.

George had also just stood after rubbing the second fiend's face into the sidewalk like sandpaper and snapping the first's neck. Aware of the moans and caterwauls coming from down the street as he fought, he'd done his best to make quick work of his two opponents.

He'd also heard the boys screaming and spotted the impending attack. There was no time to count how many ghouls were coming. All he knew was that there were too many. Megan was standing next to him with a dazed expression on her face and blood on her hands. The body at her feet told the desperate man all he needed to know. Jason and Teddy were still waving frantically at them as they followed Lydia and the children between two small office buildings across the street.

Making a quick decision, George pushed Megan in their direction.

"Go! Get out of here! NOW!"

His words snapped Megan out of her daze as she stumbled back. George knew that was all he could do for her as he turned to face the first attacker. The big man's meaty fist shot out, dislocating the nurse's jaw. The cannibal jittered sideways and fell to the ground. As three more monsters lunged at him, their teeth gnashing, George let out an enraged howl and body checked them into the next group of ghouls coming his way.

As he waded into a mass of monsters, he screamed at the others.

"Get them the hell out of here. I'll hold these things off as long as I can!"

His arms were a blur as George drove his elbow into the temple of one of the people tearing at his clothing. He whirled around, bumping another malnourished form to the ground.

As more of the townsfolk of Manchester closed in on him, their howls and screeches filled with inhuman rage, George spied Megan backpedaling. Lydia and the children were already out of sight, along with Teddy, but Jason was standing near the opening of the alleyway, his eyes filled with horror as he watched what was happening to George.

"I'm right behind you!" George shouted as he lashed out with his foot and turned away from his friends. He tried to repeat the words, but they were cut off as a small wriggling body smashed into him. The big man lifted the rancid child above his head and launched it at two more stiffening forms coming straight at him.

George growled as he twisted away from another set of shattered teeth that snapped and gnashed at him. All he could see was gray, putrid flesh and milky white eyes as more and more hands tried to pull him to the ground.

As he continued to fight, images of his family flashed through his mind. They seemed farther away now than ever. The people he'd met over the past few days were all too real, but his wife and two daughters seemed like nothing more than a dream.

Shaking away the despair that threatened to take hold of

him, George gritted his teeth as he landed another punch and broke free from a throng of bodies.

"I'm still coming for you, babe. No matter what, I'm still coming for you and the girls."

It was all he managed to say as he barreled into another pile of corpses.

Chapter 8

Megan picked up her pace and urged Jason to keep up. He kept looking back as if expecting George to come running up behind them. She urged the kid on, but was careful not to jar his injured elbow.

They caught up with Teddy and Lydia, and Megan took hold of the two small boy's hands as she slowed her pace to match the others. She refused to think about what George had done for them. She had already lost Jeff, and thinking about both of them being gone was too much to bear. Instead, she needed to focus on the task at hand: the remaining survivors had to get off the street and find a place to hide as soon as possible.

The others slowed down and bunched up behind Megan as they hit the end of the alley. They were looking out on another street. Taking a deep breath, the new leader of the group motioned for her charges to follow. Noise was cascading down from all sides, distant cries mixed with closer sounds from where they had left George.

The street onto which they moved was lined with low-slung buildings of various configurations. Several free-standing offices and storefronts made of wood, aluminum, and brick dotted the road. Megan spotted a door across the way that appeared to be made of steel and looked sturdier than the rest. It was one of several entryways in the building, but the others were all made of decorative glass or wood. The gold-trimmed paint on the steel door spelled out a name, though much of it was covered in filth and was hard to read. All Megan knew was that if it was unlocked, the sturdy door and what lay beyond might present the desperate group with a secure hiding place.

The seven human shapes scurried across the street, their panic not lessening when they saw no one nearby, since the echo of agonized moans still surrounded them.

***

As the frantic refugees moved out of the alley and onto the street, a shadow separated from one of the walls behind them and followed. Its excitement was palpable as it narrowed the distance to its prey.

The creature had been following them for some time. It ignored George as he was swarmed and kept tracking the group now composed exclusively of women and children. They were a far more tantalizing target.

It hissed in anger as the small group entered an abandoned office on the opposite side of the street. As the last of the survivors stepped inside and shut the door, the shadowy figure licked its lips greedily.

There was noise coming from farther down the alleyway, behind it. The others were getting close, but that didn't matter. They would not get there in time to interfere.

The shadowy creature crept across the street.

Chapter 9

Michael wiped the sweat from his eyes, the rifle heavy in his arms. The heat was an oven blast he'd not gotten used to, but quietly endured. Lack of water was taking its toll, along with the agony of his injury as he continued limping forward. The excited moans that had accompanied Frank's final agony had faded fast. The undead were on the hunt again. But even if those beasts remembered he existed after their feast, they would have no idea where he had gone.

The injured man kept moving, changing directions more than once to throw the hunters off his trail. He'd seen none of them for quite some time and relaxed a little.

Despite the increasing pain in his ankle and the thick, humid air that clogged his lungs, Michael dared to feel good about things. As he strolled along the city sidewalk, he knew it wouldn't be long before he could purge this hellhole from his memories and put it behind him. He would find a car and drive right out of this place. There were plenty of abandoned vehicles from which to choose, he just had to find one with the keys still in the ignition. He resisted the urge to whistle, instead allowing a small smile to cross his lips.

The attack from behind came as a complete shock.

The four children hiding in the rusted bed of the pickup truck piled high with junk rose up as Michael passed, detecting his scent on the air after having remained immobile for several days. It took less than a second for the first to launch his little body like a sluggish missile up over the side of the old Dodge and directly at Michael.

The minor blow to his back knocked him off balance and forced Michael to put weight on his bad ankle, twisting it as he tried to overcompensate. A howl of agony burst from his lips as he crashed to the ground, writhing in pain.

The boy plopped down next to Michael, who clutched his ankle, his vision dimming. Realization of what was happening came quickly, and the man rolled over, his ankle held tight to his body. Clenching his teeth as he continued rolling away from grasping hands, he looked up in time to see a second child, smaller than the first, diving off the edge of the truck toward his exposed torso. At the same time, two other heads popped up over the side of the truck, mouths smeared with blood. Michael deflected the girl's descent toward him with an elbow to the ribs. He pushed up hard, and the miniature revenant bent in the middle, her legs flopping wildly as she skidded backwards across the pavement.

Michael snatched up his rifle, which had clattered to the ground during the opening attack. He drove the metal muzzle through the left eye of the next child who dove at him, skewering the creature like a fish. Pushing the weapon and its impaled victim away, he followed up the assault with an elbow smash to the first assailant, who was creeping closer. The blow connected with the child's forehead and drove its head into the cement. Michael ignored the crunching noise and the stench that erupted from the young boy's shattered skull as he detected a wet plopping sound a few feet away. He turned to see that the fourth child, the most ravaged of the bunch, had managed to drag its maimed carcass over the side of the truck, but had the misfortune of landing head first on the edge of the curb. The pathetic creature's body flopped over and leaned against the rear wheel of the vehicle, motionless. Michael reassured himself it was truly dead before twisting to face his single remaining opponent. The little girl had skidded to a halt a few feet away, but was back on her feet. The initial blow to her chest had likely cracked a few ribs, though she was unfazed by the damage. She charged at him, pigtails bouncing.

Michael met the child's rush on his knees. In a fluid motion, he gripped both sides of her skull as she got close. Without so much as a cringe at the rotten-apple mushiness beneath his hands, the ruthless killer twisted the girl's neck violently. The doll-like arms, extended to embrace him, did a jittery dance and flopped to her sides. A sound like crunching peanut shells told Michael all he needed to know, and he dropped the feather-thin body to the ground.

Growling in pain, he grabbed his rifle, wrenching it free from the eye socket of the boy he had speared. Using it like a crutch, he climbed back to his feet. As the exhausted survivor rose up, his stomach roiled from an overload of pain in his leg.

Michael surveyed his handiwork. Three dead children and one paralyzed from the neck down. The little girl stared up at him balefully, her body and appendages useless.

"I hope you live forever, you little cunt," he spat at her.

Lifting his head, Michael blotted the children out of his mind and listened intently. He cursed and resumed limping down the street.

Those things had heard his scream. They were coming for him again.

It only took a couple of minutes for the infected in the immediate area to tighten the noose around Michael, who was forced to open fire with the M16 once again. Breathing raggedly, the harried man picked his shots carefully, skipping targets not directly impeding his forward progress. With every step, his wounded ankle felt like it was being dipped into molten lava, but he knew he couldn't stop for any reason. Even as he took a risk and turned a blind corner around a building in an effort to confuse his pursuers, there was no slowing up, not even to catch his breath.

The bullets were gone quickly, the second clip evaporating faster than the first. A dry click marked the end of the ammo, and Michael immediately changed course again, swerving away from a ghoul that had been in his crosshairs. Weaving between buildings, he was positive he was getting close to escaping downtown Manchester. Moments later, as he moved in front of a little market, he spied a small stand of trees up ahead.

Nearly weeping with relief, the desperate renegade counted only a few more retail establishments standing between him and the suburban landscape. Grunting in pain, Michael picked up his pace. The noise had faded behind him, and he hoped that his tortuous path had confused his pursuers, if only for the time being.

Just a few more buildings to go: an auto parts store, a hair salon, a drug store, and a bank. Past that, it would be far easier to see anything coming for him. Fewer mangled vehicles, ruined bodies, and piles of ash to contend with. Michael couldn't see any houses, just trees, but there had to be a neighborhood nearby. He was sure the air was starting to smell better, cleaner somehow. The haze from the heat rising from the asphalt would be gone soon as well. Soon. Very soon.

That was when the two teens slithered from their hiding place just inside the grocery store vestibule. Michael saw them out of the corner of his eye and barely had time to raise the rifle to which he still clung possessively before they tackled him. He toppled over, the M16 the only thing separating him from the teeth of the boy above him. The other ghoul, a girl, collapsed on top of the two combatants. Her eyes bulged with excitement as she reached for Michael.

Panic took over, and Michael scrambled frantically in an attempt to break free of the gibbering piles of flesh groping him. Teeth snapped at his clothes, and clawed hands pawed at his exposed flesh. He didn't hear the distressed cry that broke free from his lips as he drove his rifle forward with a surge of strength born of desperation. Michael somehow managed to wriggle free of his two attackers and, from his position on the ground, lashed out with his good leg. There was a huff of air as his foot connected with something solid. He kicked again and used the contact to push back from the two stiffs. Rolling away, he wrapped his arms around his face in an attempt to avoid getting scratched or bitten. Tucking the rifle tight to his chest, the survivor didn't stop until he was certain he was in the clear.

Slamming the M16 to the pavement, Michael pulled himself skyward. His ankle was a blast furnace sending endless signals of pain to his brain as he tried to focus. The two teens were still on the ground, their arms raised toward the living man as if asking him to help them get back to their feet.

The waves of panic rushing through Michael ebbed, and he scanned the area for other attackers. He blinked away the burning, sweaty tears from his eyes, and still saw no one. Gripping the rifle rigidly, he advanced on the prone forms. He saw the girl's eyes blaze with anticipation just before the butt of his weapon slammed down on the side of her face with a satisfying *whap!* Several teeth went flying, and the foul monster's head turned at an abnormal angle. Raising the rifle again, he brought it down repeatedly on the boy's head until the creature's ghastly eyes closed for good. A whimpering burble of agony came from deep in Michael's throat as he took the last swing.

Hands raw, Michael stared at the mangled mess the M16 had become. The barrel was bent, and the useless weapon clattered to the ground as he staggered off.

He set his sights on the bank he had seen up ahead. It was just past a hair salon, and there was an empty parking lot situated between the two buildings. The salon was a worn-down wooden building with a huge picture window out front. It looked like a giant fishbowl. The bank, on the other hand, had a brick veneer with several nooks and crannies that could provide temporary shelter while he took a short rest. That was what the exhausted warrior needed: a few moments to rebuild his strength before moving on.

Michael did not look back, but couldn't avoid hearing the sound behind him. The low rumble of vocal cords corrupted by infection seemed to be crying out for him.

The thought that he was probably the last survivor in Manchester elevated his pulse as he tried to increase his speed. His arms spun like a windmill, and he nearly fell over. Desperately righting himself, he slowed, forcing his good leg into a hopping motion.

"Let me make it … got to make it. Fuck if I'm going to die here … no way, no how," Michael hissed through dry, cracked lips. The words kept time with his hops as the gimpy man worked to maintain his balance. The pain was intense, but manageable, and he repeated his newfound mantra over and over again.

Angling toward the bank, he saw three drive-through lanes on the side of the building. He was passing the hair salon, which looked like a creaky old place where sixty-year-old matrons went to get their bouffant hairdos spruced up every other week. There was a modest sign hanging in the front window with a pair of scissors and the name 'Josie's Hair Care' on it. A bright yellow plastic sign sat on a small metal trailer out near the street. The sign had lit up at one time in the past but now was cracked and stained, years of dry rot taking its toll. As Michael limped through the salon's modest parking lot, he looked inside the dingy little shop. Beyond a cheaply paneled receptionist's desk were four empty hair-cutting stations and several hooded dryers. The place was empty, and he relaxed slightly as his eyes moved back to the bank.

The bank's recessed entrance faced the street, but was draped in shadows. There were two sets of doors, one outside and one a few feet past a vestibule leading to the lobby. All he could hope as he hobbled toward them was that both sets of doors were unlocked. If they weren't, he might have to find something out in the parking lot with which to smash the plate glass.

A quick glance behind made Michael's mind rest a bit easier. There was no one following him just yet. The distant caterwauling cries of the dead remained, but he could see no one … and hopefully no one could see him either. Only the dead teens caught his eye, but he didn't concern himself with them. The infected tended to ignore their kind, dead or alive. Apparently virus-tainted flesh didn't appeal to their taste buds.

Michael's relief was palpable as he turned back toward the

bank, but he nearly fell over in shock as he stopped short.

"You have got to be kidding me."

Creeping around the far corner of the bank was a hick in tight blue jeans. Michael froze, his nerves fried. His eyes darted from side to side as he looked for a way to avoid the redneck pusbag meandering toward him. He looked wistfully toward the bank entrance and noticed that the ghoul's eyes followed the movement.

Taking a deep breath, Michael carefully moved forward. The hillbilly was dragging a wounded leg that mimicked his own injury.

You can handle one. Just one more of these bastards. Get rid of it quickly, and things will be okay.

"So what do they call you? Billy Bubba?" the injured man hissed between his teeth, the words dripping with disdain.

The grim specimen let out a noise that sounded more like a belch than a moan, and Michael snarled in anger. The noise carried, echoing off the bank walls. It would certainly draw attention.

As he moved closer, the stiff matched him stride for decrepit stride. Billy Bubba had the obligatory mullet, molester mustache, and sleeveless t-shirt allowing a clear view of a series of tasteless and poorly drawn tattoos running up and down his arms. He shuffled forward, his slow, stiff-legged gait looking natural and unforced. Despite the ragged bite wounds on his upper thigh and his pale gray skin, Michael guessed that death hadn't changed much about old Billy.

He stopped short of the ghoul's outstretched arms and assumed a defensive stance. They were close to the darkened entrance of the bank, and Michael knew his best hope was to take the ghoul out quickly and then head for the doors.

Recalling the moves he had learned from four years of studying Tae Kwon Do, he made a circular motion with his left hand. The side of the appendage connected with the ghoul's cheekbone. Michael bent his elbow, moving his fist toward his own body and then quickly lashing out, slamming the back of it into the other side of Billy's face. The living man's other hand flew out with a straight jab to the bridge of the rotter's nose. There was a satisfying crunch of bone, and the monster rocked backwards.

Michael sighed when Billy grinned at him through shattered black teeth. The crushed nose was no deterrent. There wasn't even any blood leaking out of the smashed remains of the stiff's beak. All it did was add to the gruesome charm of the determined predator.

Michael's knuckles ached, but he ignored the pain and attempted another move. Unfortunately for him, a fake jab did not elicit the hoped-for response. Billy didn't even blink as Michael's left hand stopped short of the hick's face while his other hand struck him in the temple. The blow knocked the creature's head to the side, but Billy wasn't deterred, and his momentum carried him into Michael, driving the injured man backwards on his bad leg as they crashed to the ground together. Even as they were falling, Billy's greedy eyes stayed focused on his prize.

Michael tensed his shoulders to keep his head from smacking the pavement, and his back exploded in pain as air rushed from his lungs. The full weight of Billy wasn't impressive, but Michael felt a slicing sensation in his back as several of his ribs cracked.

Despite the white-hot pain, Michael couldn't scream. He forced his forearm underneath the ghoul's chin as he tried to catch a breath. Billy's fingers clawed at his arms and face as the foul demon hissed and drooled. Cracked and tar-colored teeth were inches from Michael's eyes.

He fought the urge to puke as a powerful graveyard stench poured over him. A hand grasped his shoulder, the ragged, broken nails digging into his thick camo jacket. Grunting, Michael pushed up on Billy's throat. There was a snap, and the hissing noise suddenly stopped as the ghoul's esophagus closed off, but the damage didn't deter Billy. Another wave of nausea washed over Michael as the pain in his back took on an immediacy that had not been there before.

Shaking off the mitt pawing at his shoulder, Michael deflected Billy's other hand as it came up to tear at his face.

He planted his good foot on the asphalt and managed to thrust the rotting ghoul back several feet. A searing flash of pain ricocheted through Michael's head, and his vision swam, but a surge of adrenaline allowed him to scramble over to the edge of the building. Dragging his hands across the brick surface, the bruised and battered man pulled himself to a standing position.

Fighting to stay conscious, Michael stared at the ghoul. It was trying to lever itself back to its feet, but its gimpy leg was prolonging the process. Billy attempted a growl, and all that came out through his wounded throat was a bubbling hiss. Michael shook his head in frustration. The rotting bastard looked no worse for wear, while the survivor was deteriorating quickly. It was time to finish things.

The knife plowed into Billy's left eye socket just as he got to his feet. There was a small popping sound as the blade ruptured his eyeball and sliced into his brain. A small amount of vitreous humor trickled onto the knife as Michael twisted the blade for good measure. He snarled as he did so, reaching for Billy's mullet to get a better grip. When the blade snapped off at its base, Michael relaxed his fingers, and the ghoul slumped sideways to the ground. The body twisted, and Billy landed face up. The victor stared down at his handiwork, and Billy stared back up at him with his one remaining eye.

A few moments later, the world came crashing in on Michael. He fought to stay on his feet as he shook with weakness. It was tempting to remain standing where he was and wait for more of those monsters to come for him. It didn't matter anymore; he was all used up. But with the last bits of his rational mind that remained, he realized that he still wanted to survive. Wheezing, he wrapped an arm around his midsection and dragged his body toward the bank entrance.

As he pushed on the metal door handle, tears burned at the corners of Michael's eyes. It creaked in tired protest but swung inward, and he nearly toppled forward, caught off balance. He hiccupped in disbelief at his good luck, his tears mixing with a muffled laugh as the door swung wide, granting him access to the vestibule.

Dust swirled as though furious at being disturbed, caking Michael's exposed skin with a grungy sprinkling of dirt. He moved forward, and his hand touched one of the inside doors. The bank lobby beyond looked cool and inviting, not the least bit frightening.

The door resisted his effort, and Michael crashed into it, unable to check his momentum. It rattled in protest but didn't budge. He turned, pressing his back against the locked doors as he slid to the floor. He felt a sharp pain from his cracked ribs as he leaned back.

As the pounding of blood in Michael's ears subsided, he took slow, short breaths. It was too painful to breathe any faster or deeper. When he did, it felt like daggers were being driven deep into his back.

He looked out the glass doors to the world beyond and snarled. "I'm still alive, you fuckers. You haven't gotten me yet."

He sat and listened. They were getting closer. Looking up, Michael confirmed that there was no deadbolt, just a keyhole lock on the exterior doors. He shifted his body, enduring the agony of the movement until his good foot, with its solid black boot, was wedged in front of the seam between the outer doors while his back was flat against the inner doors. He gasped in pain, his exhaustion from the effort acute.

The noise outside was getting louder, and Michael giggled. It started deep in his throat, and he covered his mouth when it became uncontrollable. More tears rolled down his face, and he could feel his mind slipping away.

He was as much of a gimp as he had turned Frank into. At least with Frank it took a knife to do it. All the damage to Michael's body had been caused by his own stupidity. He looked at his right foot, swollen inside his boot, and the giggles rained down. Each laugh brought a stab of pain to his back. But he couldn't help it.

"Sorry, Frank. God, I'm sorry. For whatever it's worth."

The words brought another laughing jag. He couldn't figure

out if he was trying to pray to Frank or to God. Not that either one was listening. And for whatever reason, that was hilarious to Michael.

There wasn't any point to asking for forgiveness. Michael knew he could never apologize for all the pain he'd inflicted on the people who had relied on him, and he had no desire to do so. No, he was hell bound, if there was such a place, and that suited him just fine. A grin split his face. Hell would be a vacation compared to this place.

His eyes were still closed when he heard a fist banging on the door.

Chapter 10

The bat bent on the second swing, the thick aluminum splitting and folding in on itself.

Jeff rubbed his hands gingerly. The ghoul had already been sliding down the brick wall when his swing connected with the corner of the building right above its head, sending unpleasant vibrations up and down his arms.

A decorative splat of gore remained on the bricks as the remains of the stiff hit the ground. Jeff glanced at his bat before tossing it away in frustration. It was time to find another weapon.

He had snuck in between a dumpster and the back wall of a fast food joint moments before. He'd been running in circles trying to track the gunfire while avoiding the clumps of infected scattered all over town. They were spread much thinner than at the RV wreck, and only a few had spotted him so far. He had taken care of those few, just like the one on the ground next to him, which had wandered too close as it chased a rat into the parking lot.

Jeff froze. The sharp scream was the only sound other than moaning that he had heard in fifteen minutes. It was short, full of surprise and pain. Nothing like the prolonged cry of agony he'd heard earlier. This sounded like someone had been taken off guard.

There was a response out on the street to the scream. The rotters out front grew excited and moved with purpose toward the sound.

Leaning against the dingy metal door at the back of the restaurant, Jeff stared past the drive-through menu board. The scream had come from down the street. He stood silently for another minute listening as growls, moans, and the occasional high-pitched whimper floated past his position. The bulk of the noise came from in front of the restaurant, but he caught a few stray sounds that were hard to pinpoint. A fence that ran along the back of the restaurant parking lot and past several other lots would hopefully keep the stiffs from creeping up behind him.

Jeff stood waiting, gnawing on one of his fingernails. He spit out a sliver of nail and moved on to the next. This was his fourth nail in the last half hour. He could feel the guilt curdling in his stomach. He'd been able to escape the large group of stiffs that had chased him away from the RV, but hadn't turned back around once he was in the clear. Instead, he had heard the gunfire and followed it, like some bloodhound tracking a scent. And now he was far too twisted around and lost to find his way back to the RV. Not that he suspected the others were anywhere close to the wreck anymore. With any luck, they'd gotten as far away from that area as possible. He would search for them later ... after he was sure Michael didn't present a threat to them anymore.

When the gunshots resumed a few moments later, spaced out but steady, the noise broke Jeff's reverie, and he knew it was time to get moving again.

The gunfire continued, and the infected moved with it, lured forward. It wasn't coming from too far away. Jeff's heart raced as he abandoned his hiding spot and ran toward the fence.

He looked back toward the street, pausing to make sure no one saw him climb the rusty chain link. Spotting another fence off in the distance a few lots away, he ran toward it.

For the next ten minutes, Jeff plotted a course parallel to the ghouls, sneaking behind buildings and climbing fences not only to keep up, but to get ahead of the pack. When he was sure he had gained a sufficient lead and the coast was clear, he worked his way back toward the street.

That was when he saw the two corpses lying on the ground. Their skulls had been caved in, and black ooze was still dripping onto the asphalt from the fresh wounds.

He scanned the immediate area and noticed something nearby. Moving closer, he bent over the twisted remains of a military rifle. As he ran his fingers along its metal surface, his lips curled into a dark smile.

Chapter 11

"FUCK YOU!"

Michael braced his foot as the doors vibrated beneath it. He stiffened his body as the two ghouls spit and lashed out from outside his glass prison. Each time they bashed on the frame or pushed against the doors, his back clenched up, and his broken ribs stabbed at his lungs. Yelling seemed to help. It was something he'd been unable to do much of over the past few weeks, and being granted the freedom to bellow with abandon felt liberating, despite the circumstances.

The two defectives looked nearly as bad as Michael felt. Their skin was cracked and peeled, separating from the bone while glistening fluids oozed from their wounds. As they slammed and scraped against the door, chunks of nerveless tissue broke free of their bodies and slid down the glass.

Another ghoul joined them, and Michael's frustration turned into hopelessness. The woman, whose torn face showed the full extent of her dental work, had her hair cropped into the signature style of a soccer mom. She was dressed comfortably in a pair of athletic shoes, jeans, and a form-fitting t-shirt, which showed off what might have been an attractive figure before she was transformed by the virus into a freak show.

With a scream filled with determined anger and agony, Michael shifted his body. The pain in his back nearly caused him to faint, but he refused to give up. He slid one of his hands behind him and pressed it up against the inner doors.

He gently dragged his twisted ankle until his knee was bent and pushed his weight upwards. His other foot remained firmly wedged against the outer doors as beads of sweat popped up all over his body. If he could turn around ... maybe there was a way to stand without letting the doors crash open.

His injured ankle gave way, and Michael cried out as he tumbled down. His elbow crunched on the floor and prevented his back from slamming into the wall. The pain from bracing his body stung, but was overridden by other agonies. Tears rolled down the man's face as he slammed his fist into the thin, musty floor mat in frustration.

The movements had his admirers frothing at the mouth. The rain of blows grew more frantic, desperate in their insistence. He ignored them and shifted back into the most comfortable position he could muster with his foot still wedged in place.

"So this is it, huh? I get to spend my last minutes on earth with you three cocksuckers? Just great. Just fucking great."

Michael took slow shallow breaths as he looked around the vestibule. There was nothing of interest in it. There was a framed poster bolted to the wall, which advertised new higher interest rates on CDs, but nothing that might help.

He resisted another concerted effort by the three rotters to break in. The glass showed no signs of damage; there was not a single crack in it, and Michael wondered if it were shatterproof.

He also wondered how much longer he could hold out.

His good leg remained stiff as he pressed on the door, but with each violent thud, it was weakening, the tremors hammering him mercilessly. If just one more of those things came to the door, he was done for.

Michael let the moments slide by as he thought about what would happen if he just gave up. The infected wouldn't leave him alone. They would stay here as long as it took for him to either give up or grow weak enough that he couldn't hold the door shut anymore. Being stuck in this stiflingly small space like a rat in a trap was not the answer.

Michael let his knee relax, just a bit. The doors inched inward with each jarring blow. They would swing back into place for an instant, and then another meatless fist would paste itself on the glass, pushing the doors farther inward each time.

It won't be that bad. Just a few moments of pain, then an eternity of oblivion ...

After one of the more violent blasts, Michael heard a different noise outside. Looking up, he saw smears of blood along with a few teeth splattered across the double doors. As he studied the graffiti, the face of one of the ghouls slammed into the middle of the smear. The door vibrated, but stayed closed as more crud besmirched the glass, expelled from the creature's mouth and eye sockets. It left a gooey streak until its head separated from the glass, the body's momentum pulling it away as it crumpled to the ground, immobile.

The other two stiffs lost interest in the door as they turned to respond to whatever had bashed their cohort's skull in.

Michael watched in amazement as a blow came down on the head of the soccer mom. Through the smudged and blurred glass, he saw her legs quake then collapse beneath her. The blow was strong and precise, exerted with tremendous force. Someone still breathing was out there.

The third rotter moved out of Michael's field of vision. The injured man pulled his leg back and leaned on his elbows. He heard a hollow thud and what sounded like a sack of laundry being dumped to the ground.

Still stunned at the sudden change in his situation, Michael inched backwards, his good leg pushing until he was propped up comfortably against the inside doors again.

His mind raced with possibilities as he shrank back against the wall. He knew the odds were not in his favor that whoever was out there would be friendly to him.

Roaring in pain, he tightened his fists as he worked to pull his leg up underneath him. With an agonizing twist of his body, he reached for a door handle and rose to his feet. Shifting until he was leaning against the inner door, Michael hoped that whoever was outside would not immediately realize how banged up he was.

A shadow crossed the door. Michael tensed as he saw a hand reach for the handle. It was impossible to catch a glimpse of who it was past the befouled glass. The door moved inward.

"Jeff?"

He blinked at the question and stared out at the person who had asked it.

"Michael ... is that you?"

Michael's mouth moved silently as he attempted to form words. He was shocked. Standing before him was not the person he'd expected.

George stepped into the vestibule, his eyes wide with shock.

Chapter 12

George could barely remember what had happened to him.

The battle with the pack of ghouls had been intense, and he'd been running on pure adrenaline the entire time. The last thing he remembered was breaking free of the crowd and running. His clothing was torn, but he had not been bitten and was able to lead the stiffs on a wild goose chase. It was touch and go for a while, yet he somehow managed to escape. When there was a moment to rest, he realized he was completely lost. Looking for any landmarks that might lead him back to the others, he instead discovered a trail of bodies.

Hearing gunfire up ahead, he ignored it, hoping the beaten bodies of the children next to the truck indicated that someone without a gun, perhaps Ben or Jeff, was responsible for their demise. A little while later, when George saw the two mangled teenagers and heard several stiffs beating on the bank doors, he was certain he'd found one of the other two men. So instead, when he saw the man who had done everything he could to prevent George from getting back to his family, he was livid.

***

"You unbelievable bastard."

Michael smiled. It helped hide his surprise while he attempted to wrap his head around the fact that the big lummox standing before him was alive.

"George. Now is that any way to say hello to an old friend?"

George glared at him. "You're no friend of mine. I should

kill you where you stand."

Michael *tsked* and shook his head as his smile widened. The cold fear he felt when he first saw George had shrunk to a manageable lump in the pit of his stomach.

"George, George, George. What good would that do? Look, we're both big boys here. Time is short. Why don't you just step aside and let me pass?"

Michael raised his hands to show he was unarmed. "Nothin' up my sleeves, George. I did all I could to survive until now, but I'm not in real great shape. So why don't you just let me head out that door and on down the road? I swear you'll never see me again."

He watched the hulking figure standing before him, and when George didn't respond, Michael moved forward, carefully balanced on his good foot. When George shifted to block the exit, Michael stopped, fighting hard to remain standing.

"You're not going anywhere."

Michael's eyes widened in anger. He was tired. Tired of dealing with both the living and the dead, and this oversized bastard and his misguided sense of nobility were starting to piss him off.

"So what the fuck are you going to do, George? Are you going to stop me? I've had enough bullshit for one day. Enough bullshit for a lifetime. Now get out of my way."

The hand shot out faster than Michael could see. The flat of George's palm sent him reeling back into the glass doors. Crying out in pain, Michael lost his balance and fell to the ground.

"You're going to pay for what you did to us ... for what you did to Ray."

Michael looked up at George, who was now crowding him. The shock of how fast the oversized lump could move was wearing off as anger bleached the pain away.

"Fuck you, old man. The boy was going to die anyway. It was a mercy kill, and you know it. All you weak, whiny bitches wanted to do was waste time crying over him as he turned into one of those things. You've got a lot of fucking nerve trying to judge me just because you didn't have the balls to kill him yourself."

He spit at George, but the wet glob got no higher than his knee.

"You're all fucking pathetic. You don't have a clue what it takes to survive. You just want to cling to how things used to be and how they used to work." Michael's eyes were on fire, and he shook with anger. "That ain't how it is anymore, George! But you're just too fucking stupid to see the truth. I'm the only one who's figured it out. Until you morons came along and screwed everything up."

Michael clenched his fists and pounded the floor as he cursed.

"Pathetic. You're all pathetic."

George stooped lower and narrowed his eyes at Michael, his nostrils flaring.

"I could just kill you." It sounded like an offer, and Michael's eyes widened. "Or maybe I should let those poor confused people out there find you, after I snap both of your legs so you can't get up and leave." George paused and moved back as he tried to reign in his emotions. "But I'm not going to do that. I'm going to take you back to the others. So we can decide how you should be punished."

Laughter sputtered out of Michael's mouth. It lasted a few moments before he looked up and saw the surprise on George's face. He began to clap. His laughter grew stronger, like the uncontrollable giggles from earlier. It hurt his ribs, but he couldn't resist the urge to mock the dumb bastard.

Michael knew he had lost his sense of reality. Sanity these days was a very subjective thing. You had to be at least a little bit 'off' to still be alive. Very few sane people had lasted past the first week after the dead had risen. But some of the survivors had lost *all* depth perception. That was George. He had no perspective on reality whatsoever.

When he could finally catch his breath and stop laughing, Michael tried to explain things to the puzzled man above him. "I know I said you were pathetic ... but I didn't realize how pathetic. You just don't get it, do you, George? There isn't going to be any war crime tribunal, and I'm not going to be sentenced to twenty-five to life, you dumb fuck!"

George grabbed Michael's shoulders and shook him hard. "You're the one who's pathetic, Michael! I don't give a shit what you think. You're coming with me to face your punishment."

Michael's smile did not fade, despite the strong fingers digging through his jacket and into his skin.

"George, I'm kind of wondering where you plan on taking me. Don't tell me someone else made it out of that busted-up bus alive? Pretty nifty trick. So where are they now? All shacked up at the Ritz-Carlton?"

George shook Michael again, eliciting a grimace as he snarled. "Shut up! You thought we all died back there, didn't you? We didn't! We got out of there in spite of what you did, you fucking coward! We made it out alive!"

Michael gawked at George, his mind swimming. He didn't think the man was capable of bluffing about something like that, but what he said didn't make sense. He shook his head.

"I don't think so, George. Why would you be here alone if everyone else is alive? Why wouldn't you be with them?"

"Shut up! It doesn't matter what you think. What does matter is that I'm going to drag you out of here, by your hair if necessary!"

The pain in his back was acute, and the broken ribs were digging deeper into his lungs, but Michael fought through the pain and guessed at what must have happened after he fled the RV with Cindy and Frank.

"You ran away from them, didn't you, George? You left them all to die somewhere, right? Those things were coming for you, they were closing in-"

George slammed him back again, and Michael's head hit the glass, leaving his ears ringing. George was yelling at him, a string of curses flying from his mouth, but in his dazed condition, Michael couldn't quite hear them all.

As George continued his denial about leaving the others behind, Michael's head began to clear, and his eyes narrowed as he thought of something else.

"So you saw Cindy then?"

The words sliced through George's rant with the precision of a scalpel. He cut off mid-word when he heard the woman's name.

"What?" George's brow furrowed as he tried to puzzle out why Michael was asking about Cindy.

"Cindy, man! Cindy. Don't you remember her? My mean-ass bitch of a girlfriend with all the freaky tattoos? She left the RV with Frank and me, but got some wild hair up her ass and decided to turn back." Michael shifted his head thoughtfully, as if he had just recalled another critical detail. "I think it had something to do with taking care of some unfinished business with you fine upstanding folks."

George's mouth opened, shut, and opened again. Michael resisted the temptation to cackle. Instead, he knew he had to slip the knife in just a bit deeper. Twist it around a bit.

"Oh ..." Michael took on a look of mock surprise. "So you didn't see Cindy, huh? Well, she must have met up with the others after you abandoned them. I'm sure you juuust missed her."

George still looked confused.

"George. George?" Michael snapped his fingers. George had been staring off into space as he tried to sort out what he was being told. "What does that matter anyway? Those people aren't your responsibility, now are they?" George's confused look changed slightly. Michael's words were no longer harsh or snide. They sounded almost sympathetic.

"It really doesn't matter what Cindy plans on doing to them, does it? What does matter is your family, right?"

The confusion in George's eyes faded as his jaw clenched. He glared down at his prisoner.

Michael *tsked* again. "It's a goddamned tragedy when a man can't take care of his own. All this time spent tending to Jason and Megan when you should have been with your family, not a bunch of fucking worthless refugees. And now they're probably dead because you fucked up. It's a downright shame."

The hands slammed into Michael's throat before he could

react. He brought his knee up, attempting to drive it into George's groin. It missed as the big man shifted forward, and the blow glanced off of his leg instead. Michael brought his hands up at the same time, grabbing at the meaty paws wrapped around his neck.

He scratched at the tightening hands threatening to crush his windpipe, dragging his fingernails across the skin, leaving deep gouges in it. Michael pushed up on George's face, scratching him there as well, trying to shove him away. Nothing seemed to work. The hands were too strong, and Michael's airway was closing off. It was not long before his struggles slowed and spots wavered before his eyes.

Michael had been supremely confident that George was a gutless worm and would crumble when push came to shove, but as he started blacking out, it was painfully and belatedly obvious how wrong he was.

He didn't feel the hands around his throat relax or the weight of George's body disappear above him. All Michael knew was that he could breathe again. He coughed violently and sucked in huge gouts of air. The strangling victim's vision swam back into focus, and he gingerly touched at the bruises around his throat.

When he could finally see clearly again, Michael looked at George, who was leaning against the wall with his face in his hands. He wasn't quite sure, but he thought the big oaf was crying.

As he tried to breathe normally, or at least what passed for normally with broken ribs and a mangled throat, Michael hissed painfully and shifted his wrecked body. Reaching for the door handle for a third time, he began the arduous task of lifting himself off the ground once again.

He heard the hitching of George's chest and couldn't help but smile. The old man didn't have the guts to kill him, just as he had suspected. The new bruises on his neck stung, though Michael knew he would be able to walk through the bank doors and George wouldn't do anything more to stop him. The pathetic loser just didn't have it in him.

Listening, Michael heard no nearby moaning—at least not

any more than before. And after all he had been through, he was willing to take his chances outside once again. He'd been given a reprieve and intended to take full advantage of it. Limping over to the outer doors and putting his hands on them, he looked back at George one last time.

"Don't let it stress you out, man. There are plenty of guys who don't have the balls to kill someone. That doesn't make you a pussy." Michael paused, savoring the moment. "But not taking care of your family ... now that makes you a pussy."

He turned, his evil grin growing even wider. He was ready to face the world again.

The grin faded as he pushed the doors open, contorting and twisting into a fearful grimace.

Jeff was standing outside with a gun in his hand. Michael stared at the weapon and didn't recognize it. It was some sort of small semiautomatic.

Michael shook his head in disbelief. Jeff was supposed to be dead. That had been made obvious when it was George who came bursting through the door. Jeff had died back at the RV with all the others. He wasn't supposed to be here.

Michael's lips moved, but he couldn't do anything more than shape the word 'No' silently.

"George might not be able to kill you, but I sure as hell can."

The first shot struck Michael's cheek. He reached up to touch the spot where the hole was, not quite sure what had happened, his head still shaking in denial. The second shot tore through his throat, and the small bullet lodged in his spine, paralyzing him from the neck down. Before he fell, there was a third shot, which punched a hole in his upper dental plate, shattering two of his incisors as the bullet plowed at an upward trajectory through his sinus cavity. As Michael dipped toward the floor, the fourth shot struck him in the forehead, the bullet lodging in his brain and forcing all mental activity to cease. At the same time, Michael blinked twice, and his mouth remained open, shaped in a final 'O' of disbelief. The last two shots in the clip slammed into the dead man's body as he lay on the ground.

Jeff didn't realize the gun that had been buried in the front pocket of his jeans for the past few days was empty until he heard several dry clicks. When he did, he dropped the weapon on Michael's motionless corpse. He continued to stare at the body for the next few seconds, trying to comprehend what he'd just done.

Several loud howls from outside put an end to his reverie. The infected army was on the move. They had a new direction to head after hearing the shots, which would lead them directly to the bank. He shifted his eyes away from the body, which was preventing the outer doors of the bank from closing.

"Come on, George. We have to get out of here."

George looked at Jeff as if he didn't recognize him.

"George! We have to leave, now!" Jeff glanced out the door and then at George. "They're coming. Let's move it!"

George continued gawking at Jeff. The man showed no signs of stress or trauma. In fact, he looked downright serene. His hands, which had gripped a pistol and pulled the trigger over and over again, sinking bullet after bullet into Michael, weren't shaking.

"How could you do it? How could you kill him?" George's eyes were red with grief, and his voice was tinged with wonder. Jeff could detect the revulsion underneath, and wiped the sweat away from his forehead before answering as best he could.

"It was better than he deserved."

It was all he could say. He was too tired to argue, too exhausted to care what George thought of him at the moment. He knew exactly what he had done and was certain the guilt over his actions would gnaw at him plenty if he ever gave it a chance. But for now, all he wanted to focus on was finding the others, if they were still alive, and getting the hell out of this godforsaken town once and for all.

George hesitated a couple more seconds before taking Jeff's hand and letting him pull him to his feet. He closed his eyes as he stepped over Michael's body. For Jeff, George's willingness to reach out to him after what he'd done wasn't absolution for his sins, but it was close enough.

As they stepped out into the parking lot, Jeff asked the question whose answer he dreaded.

"What happened to the others?"

"Cindy is still alive."

Jeff stopped and turned to face George. "What?"

There was despair in George's eyes as he spoke. "Michael said Cindy is still alive. He said she doubled back to the RV after they left." He paused, the words like lead in his mouth. "I had to leave the others behind. I tried to give them a chance to get away when we were attacked. And now Cindy is after them."

"Do you think he was lying? George! Was he lying to you? Maybe just trying to fuck with your head?"

George shrugged, his eyes swimming in confusion. "I'm not ... I'm not sure." He looked at Jeff. "But I don't think so."

Jeff frowned as his mind raced with nightmarish possibilities. He had heard screams before—screams that came from the throat of someone dying. Now, after finding Michael and ending his miserable life, he had let himself believe for a moment that he was done with the man's twisted entourage. Hearing that Cindy might still be alive was like taking a sucker punch to the gut.

The sun was heading west in the sky. It would be dusk in an hour or so, and then they would be blind until morning ... if they managed to survive until then. Somehow, Jeff doubted Megan and the others would be able to make it that long if they didn't find them ... especially before Cindy did.

He took off at a fast trot with George following, sliding between the bank and the hair salon, moving to the back of the buildings. Their first priority was to get as far away from the bank as possible.

"We have to find them. Take me to where you split up."

George hesitated and then nodded. He wasn't sure if he could remember where he'd pushed Megan away as he did battle with that wretched pack of ghouls. Even if he could, it wouldn't lead them to where the other survivors were now. That could be almost anywhere.

He prayed silently as he took the lead. He wasn't quite sure where they were going, but they had to find the others, and quick. It would be getting dark soon, and Cindy was still out there, somewhere, and she was on the hunt.

***

Not too long after the two men left the bank, others came. They crept clumsily up to the building, where they smelled fresh meat.

The body lying near the entrance still had the delicate aroma of warm flesh, though the heat was dissipating. They pushed and snapped at each other as they reached down toward Michael's corpse. Little of his skin was exposed, though there was a pool of blood beneath his head. A young boy pulled at the flesh of the handsome man's face while two bloated adults clawed and ripped at the clothing blocking their access to his torso and legs. They didn't fight with the boy for the spoils as he pulled and tore at Michael's lower lip and dipped his fingers into the already emptied left eye socket. Others joined them, and Michael's clothes were torn away and his flesh along with it. The tender organs under the skin were yanked free, along with the thick meaty muscles from his legs and arms. The crowd of ravenous creatures scooped out his brains, chewed through his intestines and sucked the marrow from his bones.

In the end, nothing but his shredded clothing and boots marked Michael's passing. Not even the blood, which had dripped thickly onto the pavement. It was licked clean by those who came too late to the feast.

Chapter 13

"Get upstairs with the kids. Teddy, help me move this desk in front of the office door."

Lydia rushed to the back of the musty insurance office, ushering the children in front of her as they moved toward the stairs. The area was dark, but clear of danger. The dust was thick and covered a loveseat and the small receptionist's desk that had a grimy monitor, keyboard, and business telephone on top of it. A calendar showing July hung on the half wall behind it next to a defunct fax machine sitting on a credenza.

Megan couldn't believe their good fortune when she found the door to the insurance office unlocked. The office had been untouched by pillagers who had ransacked many of the stores and other businesses in town. Then again, there was nothing of real value in the place. Besides brochures explaining the benefits of auto, home, and life insurance, and the agent's customer files, there was little to tempt someone.

A small utility closet and washroom sat at the back of the room, and stairs led to a second-floor storage area with a small window and several filing cabinets. More important, as far as Megan was concerned, was the door at the rear of the building that would serve as a quick escape route if needed.

She ushered Jason up the stairs with Lydia and the children. Megan was stern with him when he protested that he wanted to stay below and help. His elbow had swollen up, and he could only do so much with his one working arm. It was clear he was having a hard time coming to grips with losing George, but refused to admit it.

Megan and Teddy worked quietly in the shadows. The door that led to the street was made of steel, and she thought it would hold up fairly well under attack, but that wasn't the access point into the building that worried her most.

There were two small rooms off the entry area: the insurance agent's private office and a conference room, both with large picture windows facing the street. Megan and Teddy had already dragged the loveseat in front of the conference room door and were now sliding the desk in front of the office. If the windows were smashed in, neither piece of furniture would buy them much time, but the obstacles might give them the few precious seconds needed to make their escape out the back.

Thoughts of panic crowded Megan's head as they maneuvered the desk into place. She had resisted the urge to break down crying, but it was becoming ever more difficult to hold back the scream that threatened to burst free from her lungs.

"Thank you."

Megan looked over at Teddy. The teenager was wrung out, and his eyes were dull, but he made an effort to smile at her as he spoke.

She shook her head, feeling wretched about herself. "What are you thanking me for? I haven't done anything worth being grateful for lately."

Megan regretted the words as they came out, hearing the bitterness in her tone. She knew she sounded whiny and defensive, as if daring the kid to disagree with her. Teddy's eyes focused a bit as he responded.

"Don't say that! If it wasn't for you, I'd be dead." He paused, considering. "We'd all be dead. Don't you know that?"

The force of the words surprised Megan. Her chest hitched as she studied the boy who was barely taller than she was. For the first time, she realized how handsome he was. Despite his diminutive stature, she guessed Teddy had gotten plenty of attention from the girls at school. She smiled at him.

"Thank you." It was a whisper as she moved her hand to the teenager's face and caressed his cheek. His skin was hot, and there was a layer of moisture on it. They were both drenched after moving the furniture around the room. Teddy blinked and seemed to lean into her hand, relishing the human contact.

The loud banging on the front door made them jump.

Megan moved back, a startled gasp escaping her lips as she eyed the steel door. Teddy whirled, recoiling as his eyes bulged out in fear.

Again, a heavy pounding shook the doorframe. There were two loud knocks. Megan cocked her head, puzzled. The knocks were concise, measured. It didn't sound like something one of the infected would do.

Her heart leapt. George had found them! She crossed the floor toward the door, ready to fling it open and jump into his arms.

"Please! Let me in!"

Megan's feet stopped before her body did. She swayed and then took a step back as she felt a creeping dread.

She glanced over at Teddy and could tell by the look on his face that he was feeling the same thing. His lips moved as he uttered a single word that confirmed her worst nightmare.

"Cindy?"

He spoke the name with both fear and reverence. Megan didn't nod in response, as if by doing so she would provide the last component to whatever dark spell was being cast on them. When the door vibrated again with the sound of desperate knocking, they both jumped a second time.

"Megan? Is that you in there? They're coming for me! Please! They're not far behind. I DON'T WANT TO DIE LIKE THIS! Please ... I'm sorry for everything I did to you. You have to believe me! Please, God!"

Megan shrank back as she listened to Cindy's tear-choked scream. The banging grew louder and echoed through the office. Megan put her hands over her ears and then dropped them. Ignoring the pleas wouldn't make them go away.

That was when they heard the moans. It was also when Cindy threw her body against the door and howled with fright.

"What's going on?" Jason said from behind them.

"Get back upstairs, now!"

The twelve year old stepped backwards, almost stumbling with shock at the anger in Megan's voice. Her blue eyes glowed with rage.

"Get up there and stay put, do you understand me? Do NOT come back down here again!"

Jason nodded and practically flew up the steps.

Megan turned back to the door, the brief interaction with Jason helping to jar her out of the near-catatonia-inducing fear taking hold of her. Cindy was still banging on the door, and Megan walked toward it with Teddy behind her.

"What're you going to do?"

Megan cursed under her breath and leaned against the wall, her eyes level with the door. She watched it vibrate from Cindy's efforts. She could hear the ghouls getting closer.

"Megan, please! I am soooooo sorry! I don't want to die."

There was a sudden pause, and the banging on the door stopped. Megan lifted her head up off the wall, wondering if Cindy had decided to run. The howls and catcalls were getting louder, closer.

"They're almost here! You have to let me in, NOW!"

Megan looked at Teddy and saw the pain in his eyes. Never had she heard such terror in someone's voice, and the look on the boy's face made it clear that he was scared for Cindy, no matter what kind of person she was. Besides, if Cindy really wanted in, she could simply smash one of the picture windows and climb inside.

Megan swallowed hard as she reached for the doorknob. She gave one last look at Teddy, who hesitated for a moment and then nodded, giving his reticent blessing.

She twisted the knob and flipped the deadbolt. The door crashed in on her, knocking her backwards as Cindy flew inside. Megan landed on the ground with a loud *oomph!* Surprised and stunned, she felt a pain in her back, but was already trying to get to her feet.

When she looked up, Megan realized what a horrible mistake she had made.

Cindy was an open wound. Glass fragments had pierced the entire left side of her face from scalp to jaw. There were other cuts and gashes on the exposed part of her neck, the red crust of dried blood mixing with the dark ink of her tattoos to create an eerie display of swirling demonic images. The white tank top she wore was in tatters, and the black bra underneath was in barely better shape. It looked as if the punker had been dragged face first across fifty yards of uneven pavement. Her grin showed several cracked and shattered teeth.

Cindy slammed the door shut, muffling the raucous noises outside. She turned to look at Teddy and then shifted her gaze to Megan. Her smile widened.

"Thought you could keep me outside, didn't you?"

Megan slid backwards on the thinly carpeted floor as she shook her head in denial. Cindy followed one step at a time. She turned her back on Teddy. It was clear that Megan had her undivided attention.

"Weren't going to let me in, huh? You were going to let those rotten mother fuckers eat me, right?" Cindy paused for a second, feet stationary as she licked her lips, hands sliding down her maimed midriff in an almost sensuous manner. Her eyes rolled back in her head as the psychotic witch arched her back and moaned. "The idea of getting eaten alive does sound ... tantalizing. I'll give you that." Suddenly, her eyes snapped back onto Megan. "But I think I'll enjoy watching you die even more."

The predator moved forward again. Megan whimpered and turned over, bringing her knees up underneath her. The sudden sharp pain of Cindy's fingers grabbing her by the hair elicited a piercing scream from the petite woman. Megan scrambled to get to her feet as Cindy gave a ruthless tug upward. Megan could feel her tormented scalp relinquishing chunks of hair.

"Get off of her, you fucking bitch!"

Suddenly, Megan was back on the ground. Cindy gave her a brutal push as she turned to face Teddy, who was charging at her. The boy had stood in stunned silence as Cindy barreled inside and turned on Megan, but when she grabbed his friend, something inside him snapped. He flew with a blinding rage at the woman he had despised from the instant they met. Turning to face him, she gave the teenager a lascivious grin.

As Teddy dashed toward Cindy, he didn't notice the long shard of glass she pulled out of her jeans pocket. When he crashed into her and they slammed to the ground, he barely felt the makeshift blade slide deep into his abdomen. His fingers were already around her throat as she squeezed the glass tighter, letting it cut into her palm and fingers. Teddy's eyes widened as she watched him from below. Cindy pushed her hand down in a sudden violent thrust and watched the surprise register on the boy's face. She kept pushing until the glass shattered, leaving a bloody pile of shards in her hand.

Megan, still on the ground, only heard the two bodies slam into the carpet. She rolled over, hoping Teddy had managed to subdue the madwoman.

When she heard him scream, Megan went cold. Cindy was underneath the boy, her legs wrapped around him as he struggled to break free of her tight clench. Her mouth was next to his ear, and she was whispering something into it. Teddy's struggles were already beginning to weaken.

The screams faded as Megan scrambled to her feet and rushed over to the two intertwined figures. Cindy wiped the blood from her saturated hands, smearing it on the back of Teddy's shirt.

"NO!" Megan shouted as she knelt over them and grabbed for Teddy. She desperately tried to pry the boy free, but Cindy had her legs wrapped too tightly around him.

Cindy slid her head away from Teddy's ear and glanced up at Megan. As she did, the teenager's head slumped to the floor. The psychopath smiled.

"Damn! That was good!"

Megan kept shaking her head in disbelief, but stopped fighting the crimson-drenched woman for possession of Teddy. She stumbled backwards, stunned. Another scream surged past her lips at the sound of several fists banging on the door. Unlike Cindy's measured knocks, there was nothing precise about them.

"Ah, my friends have arrived."

Megan continued to backpedal as Cindy pushed the limp teenager's body away. Gasping, Megan knew immediately that Teddy was dead. Blood was pooling around him from a ragged slice that went from his belly button down to near his groin.

Whipping her hand back and forth several times to clear it of excess blood and the tiny slivers of glass, Cindy ignored the hammering sounds as the door behind her vibrated in its frame. Instead, she set her sights on Megan.

Cindy broke into a diabolical grin and uttered one chilling syllable: "Next."

Shaking off her stupor, Megan turned and ran for the stairs. Cindy caught up with her just as she reached the railing and drove the small woman forward. Megan tripped, and her chest slammed into the steps. A painful grunt escaped her throat, but she avoided smashing her head as the wind was knocked out of her.

"Now, now, Megan. You don't want to miss all the fun, do you?"

Cindy snagged the collar of Megan's shirt and dragged her back into the room. Desperately grasping at anything that might slow their progress, Megan snagged the edge of the partition wall in the reception area and held on for dear life. Cindy ground the heel of her black sneaker into Megan's hand until she cried out in pain and let go.

Cindy flipped her over, and Megan could see a serene smile plastered to the demonic visage peering down at her.

"Why are you doing this to me? What did I ever do to you, Cindy? Why do you hate me so much?"

The words came out around hiccups and moans of pain. It hurt when Megan breathed.

Cindy shook her head, disappointed. "Shame on you, Megan. You just don't get it, do you?"

She moved her left leg up and brought her foot down on Megan's chest. Megan screamed in agony and wrapped her hands around the shoe driving into her injured ribcage, but couldn't move it. Cindy leaned down until her face was close enough for Megan to smell her sour breath.

"I hate everyone! Haven't you figured that out yet? I even hate Michael!" Cindy sneered. "Even so, I couldn't have you trying to take him away from me. No, no, NO! No bony bitch is going to touch my man!"

Cindy pushed down harder on Megan's chest. The pain was

incredible, and she was finding it hard to suck any air into her lungs. Stars flashed in front of her eyes, and she let her hands flop to her sides.

Megan felt the pressure lessen on her chest, but then Cindy was on top of her, the vile woman's crotch a few scant inches from her face. Attempting to move her arms, Megan realized she was immobilized. The young woman's muscular legs were clamped tightly around her. Cindy bent over and studied her prisoner's face. Megan closed her eyes.

"Aw, you don't want to see it coming, do you? That's fine. I was planning on plucking your eyes out anyway. That might be fun. I figure maybe I can set you loose outside with my friends and watch you run around bouncing off of them, trying to get away. That might be fun."

"You sick bitch," Megan hissed. "I never wanted your piece of shit boyfriend. Are you really that stupid?" She tried to spit on Cindy, but it missed, and drool dribbled down her chin as she gave her torturer a defiant look.

She could hear the sounds intensifying outside, though the door continued to hold up to the pummeling it was taking. Megan desperately hoped Cindy would grow angry enough to kill her quickly, so she wouldn't have to face what was on the other side of the door.

Instead, Cindy gently wiped the spittle from her victim's face. Her eyes brightened. "I knew you would come around, Megan. Given time, I knew you would put up some kind of a fight."

There was a loud crash behind them, and Cindy swiveled her neck to look at the door. She looked back down at Megan. "Not much time left. I guess I'll only get to do you. My friends will have to take care of the others."

Megan squirmed beneath Cindy's weight. She had hoped the malevolent bitch hadn't realized anyone else was with her and Teddy, but it had been a long shot. Panicking, she found the strength to push Cindy up and slide backwards underneath her at the same time, twisting her way out of the other woman's grasp and scrambling to her feet.

Cindy whipped around and tackled her, driving her back to the ground. Megan scratched at her attacker's face, driving her nails into the open wounds already there. She raked them downward, pulling off gobs of skin. Cindy roared in pain and punched Megan, sending her head rocking into the carpet.

Megan, stunned, barely heard Cindy speaking. It sounded as if she were talking underwater.

"That's the spirit!" Cindy leaned over and licked the bruise she had left on Megan's face as she dripped blood on her. Megan could only groan in pain, her head floating. Cindy plopped on top of her again, this time farther down her chest, making sure she wouldn't be thrown off her victim again.

Cindy glanced at the front door. It was buckling. She shrugged.

"Oh well. I guess it's time to get down to business." She winked at Megan. "Sorry there won't be any more foreplay."

Cindy wrapped her hands around Megan's throat and squeezed.

Though Megan was still stunned from the punch, she sensed pressure around her neck and uncomfortable weight on her chest. She raised her arms to swipe feebly at Cindy, and her eyes fluttered open. Panic set in as she registered the look of ecstasy on the face of the woman straddling her, and she thrust her hips in an effort to buck Cindy off.

"Good. Mmm, yeah, that's good. Fight it. That's the way I like it!"

Megan's face was stricken with revulsion as she realized Cindy was getting off on strangling her. Hands constricted her windpipe, yet weren't crushing it. Cindy was too interested in savoring every terror-filled moment as she thrust her pelvis against her captive's chest and moaned with pleasure. Megan wanted to scream, but didn't have the breath to do so.

Cindy watched with a morbid fascination as her victim's eyes bugged out and her struggles became weaker. The sadistic woman was so wrapped up in her task that the noises at the door faded into dull background noise as the satisfaction from causing Megan pain crashed into her like waves of ecstasy.

That was also why she didn't hear the footsteps coming up behind her.

Lydia grabbed Cindy by the hair and yanked her head back

with her left hand. In her right was the straight razor she'd used to shave Jeff that morning. With ruthless efficiency, she cut Cindy's throat from earlobe to earlobe.

Cindy felt the sharp cut of the blade and a quick, bright pain. After the cutting ceased, there was only a cold numbness as her vision faded. Blood poured down her shirt, mixing with the gore already covering her. Splatters and ropes of it splashed Megan's face as the hands around her neck loosened. She felt Cindy's body being yanked to the side as she coughed and sucked in large gulps of air.

"Are you all right? MEGAN! Can you speak?" Lydia knelt and looked into Megan's eyes. Megan nodded, finding it hard to form words, though she was able to breathe again. The razor was gone, but blood remained on the older woman's hands, evidence of what she had done.

"We have to go! That door isn't going to hold much longer."

Megan sat up with Lydia's assistance and gawked at Cindy. Lydia had tossed her aside like a rag doll. Her lifeblood was still pouring out onto the floor beneath her open neck. She looked away, revulsion and fear clouding her thoughts. She saw Jason kneeling next to Teddy. He was weeping as he touched the boy's face.

"We have to go," Lydia repeated for the benefit of both of them. She yanked on Megan's arm, helping her to stand. "We can still get out the back door if we hurry. I didn't hear anything back there as we came down the steps."

Megan glanced down and saw the straight razor Lydia had dropped to the floor. She reached to pick it up. Ignoring the blood on the blade as she folded it, she tried to hand it back to Lydia. The older woman shook her head.

"I don't want it anymore."

Megan pushed it toward her savior and looked her in the eyes as she whispered, "We need everything we can get."

Lydia paused for a moment and then nodded. With a shaking hand, she swiped the blade back and buried it in one of her pants pockets.

Megan grabbed Lydia's arm as she tried to turn away, tried to hide the shame and anger on her face.

"Thank you."

A weak smile passed over Lydia's lips. She nodded once again and broke free of Megan's grasp, moving to the back of the building.

"I'll get the children. Get Jason."

The words came out as a croak, and Megan understood. Lydia was crying at what she had been forced to do. Megan couldn't cry, not for a life as worthless as Cindy's. Not for that animal.

She moved over to Jason. Behind her, she heard the doorframe make a sharp snapping noise. A crack had spread through the drywall surrounding the metal frame, though the steel door was still holding against the pounding.

A sound of shattering glass came from the conference room. The monsters outside had figured out an easier way in.

"Come on, Jason, we have to get out of here." Megan found herself able to put a bit of volume behind the words. Her throat felt raw, but her voice was returning despite the soreness. She reached for Jason, and he shrugged her away.

"I don't want to go. Just leave me here." He rocked back and forth over Teddy's body.

Megan leaned over the twelve year old and grabbed his good arm, pulling him around to face her.

"Jason, listen to me." Her heart raced as she heard the table inside the conference room tip over. The infected were inside the building. "We're leaving now, you and me both. I know Teddy's dead, and I don't know what's happened to George or Jeff, but I do know this much: we're still alive, and I damn well plan on keeping it that way." She gripped his arm tighter, her blue eyes flaring up as she let the anger take hold. "I won't let you make their sacrifices meaningless, just because you want to give up after all this time. Now get off your ass and move!"

Megan practically yanked him off the ground as she heard a wet slap on the hollow wooden door behind the loveseat. Jason heard it as well and watched as the door splintered. His resistance melted as the reality of what would happen if he stayed came crashing down on him.

They ran to the back of the building. Lydia was already at the door with the children and looked relieved to see them. Sadie was in her arms, and Nathan and Joey clung to her waist.

"Hold mine and Jason's hands, boys. We're going to make it out of here together!"

Megan smiled down at them. Neither smiled back, but they unlatched from Lydia and grasped the proffered hands.

Lydia put her ear to the door and listened. Satisfied, she nodded at the others.

"Let's go."

Chapter 14

Fatigue was a thing of the past and exhaustion a faint memory. Jeff could hear the wheezing of his breath in his ears and felt as though razor blades cut into his lungs with every inhalation. Desperation was the only thing that kept him moving.

They drifted from shadow to shadow, rushing from one gap or open space to another among the milling forms. They would slip into an open door or darkened entryway for a few moments until they spotted another place to which they could move. Everywhere they turned, the dreary creatures bumped and bounced against one another in agitation.

Their progress stalled as the crowds grew thicker. It felt as if they were wading into the surf against a strong current, buffeted and turned back as they were forced to shift directions time and again.

Jeff gripped the steel post he had plucked out of a gutter. It was the remnants of some road sign—a welded steel tube with perforations running down its length ending in a jagged sheared-off point that would allow him to both stab and bash. It wasn't as comfortable in his hands as the baseball bat, as its squared shape was somewhat unwieldy, but it would have to suffice.

He glanced ahead at George. As his chest rose and fell, he cursed the older man and his seemingly endless supply of energy. George had barely stopped to take a breath as he moved them through a winding path of vacant buildings and useless vehicles. The middle-aged man was physically up to the challenge of finding the others, while every muscle in Jeff's body cried out in agony.

They stopped occasionally to let George get his bearings and adjust their route. Jeff noticed that each pause was longer than the last, even if only long enough for him to gasp in exasperation as his legs begged for mercy.

As quietly as they tried to skirt the groups of the undead, Jeff was certain his heavy breathing could be heard for miles as he slogged after George. He also wondered if the stench of his sweat and bad breath might give him away. They were not feathers in the wind; they were elephants trumpeting their presence with every step.

They had already been seen from a distance, though one that was too far for the slug that watched them run by to do much about it. Still, they could hear the noises of anticipation behind them as the mob began to realize something was amiss.

The two men didn't bother looking back to see if they were being followed, keeping their eyes on the path in front of them as their feet slammed into the pavement at a rapid pace. That allowed them to deal with the two rotters that crossed their path swiftly.

George's thick plank of hardwood did one in while Jeff's newfound weapon whistled as he swung it in a downward arc onto the already fragmented skull of the other. They wasted no time studying the results as they flew past the felled bodies. So far, those two had been the only ones that had tried to intercept them. They knew their luck couldn't hold out much longer. There were just too many.

"You have ... any idea ... how close ... we are?"

The words were spaced out between Jeff's distressed breaths as they stopped behind a wrecked Mercedes that had slammed into the wall of an ice cream parlor. George's head popped up above the roof of the car to scan the roadway. After a moment, he knelt down next to Jeff.

"This is close to where I left them ... I'm pretty sure," George said, his eyes tentative as he looked around, trying to recognize any of the buildings in the immediate area.

He had seen three ghouls on the other side of the car about twenty feet away, milling around, unaware of the duo's presence. There were others farther down the street and an even thicker clot in the opposite direction. Several abandoned vehicles clogged the street and hid the two survivors from view.

George shook his head. "I don't know. They've had plenty of time to find someplace to hide. Maybe they're in one of these stores."

"Well if they were nearby and in trouble, we would probably hear something." Jeff leaned closer to George. "I mean, think about it. If they were under attack, all these dipshits would be going nuts, right?" He looked around, watching the movements of the stiffs off in the distance as he whispered. "They go ape when they find anyone."

"Unless they're already dead."

Jeff shook his head. "We can't think that way. We might as well-"

George raised a hand, cutting off the words. Jeff tensed as he moved his eyes in the direction of the other man's gaze.

The group of walkers up the street was moving their way, though it didn't appear as if they had seen the men. They weren't restless or howling in excitement. Jeff was certain they were just wandering randomly, as the infected had a tendency to do when there wasn't anything nearby to stimulate them.

They watched the progress, hearts pounding. Jeff didn't want to move. This was the longest rest he'd had since leaving Michael's bleeding corpse, though he knew they had to get rolling again soon, even if the stiffs weren't agitated by their presence.

George stood back up. "I'm going to see if the ones on the other side of the car are still there," he whispered.

Jeff nodded, taking a deep breath as he bounced up and down on his knees. He maintained his crouch, afraid to slump all the way to the ground. Getting back to his feet would be difficult enough, as exhausted as he was. His legs ached, but he wanted to be prepared as he watched George extend his body.

When George jumped back and yelped, Jeff exploded to his feet. The arm that came swinging around the rear of the car was nowhere near his friend, but the shock of the attack stunned them both. The big man crashed into Jeff, nearly knocking him off of his feet. If he had still been in a crouch, they would both have wound up on the ground. Instead, Jeff only stumbled back a couple of feet, unable to see anything with George's back in his face.

Jeff stepped to the side as he continued to backpedal. As the eclipse caused by George's broad torso was removed, he tensed at what he saw. All three pusbags were coming around the car. He gripped the metal pole with both hands and cocked his arm back.

George thrust the two by four he carried at the first ghoul, who wore a tattered cashier's uniform. Her head was already mutilated, her skull partially exposed. She rocked backwards from the jab, falling to the rear of the other two stiffs who had worked their way around her.

The metal shaft vibrated in Jeff's hands as he clocked one of the other wretches on the top of its skull. Its spindly legs collapsed underneath it even as it continued reaching for George. Hands aching from the hit, Jeff knew there would be blisters and cuts on his palms as he took a wild swing at the other, missing and slamming the pole on the top of the Mercedes. The blow hurt, but he resisted the urge to drop the weapon. The stiff ignored the swing and launched its mangled body at George.

Jeff advanced on the cashier as he heard the grunts of George battling behind him. Recuperated from the initial blow to the chin, the desiccated girl was moving toward them once again. Jeff lunged forward, jabbing the pole at her like a spear. The sharpened end struck the teen in the throat, and there was a horrible crunching noise. He relinquished his grip on the metal cylinder, which remained lodged in her throat, as she collapsed to the ground.

Darting sideways, Jeff avoided the hands of the first stiff he had clocked as it reached up for him. His blow had done little more than send it to its knees. Dodging around it, Jeff made a move for his weapon. The ghoul reached up again and fell flat on its face as the agile man slipped its grasp.

Jeff reached for the pole lodged in the cashier's throat, but recoiled. The girl's eyes were still open and staring at him, her jaw working as best it could with a shaft of metal shoved in her neck. Her arms and legs were immobile, but her eyes followed his movements.

It dawned on Jeff that his blow had paralyzed her. The point must have connected with her spine. She didn't seem to care about the injury as she glared at him balefully, her mouth opening and slamming shut like some steel-jawed trap. Repressing a shiver, Jeff wrenched the metal shaft free of her neck.

Turning, he saw the other ghoul still trying to get back up. Jeff whipped the pole around, smashing the monster's ear and knocking the ghoul flat. He bashed it in the skull again to ensure that it would not rise another time.

He was about to turn to help George when a hand slammed down on his shoulder, yanking him backwards. Tripping over his own feet, he fell to the ground as a shadow blotted out the sun above his head. As he tried to catch his breath, all Jeff knew was that it wasn't George bending over him.

Chapter 15

Tom's Donut Shop had been one of the more popular places for breakfast in Manchester. Despite the introduction of several trendy coffee shops in the area over the past few years, it had remained well trafficked up until the virus hit. Lydia led the desperate group toward the shop and away from the insurance office, which was now swarming with rotting bodies. She knew Tom's was close to the old movie palace, which had been shuttered nearly a decade before, but never torn down. If they could get to the decrepit old building and manage to find a way inside, perhaps they could hole up for a while.

They stole away from the insurance office, squirming between anonymous warehouses and boutiques, shops and office buildings, until they were at the back of the donut shop. From there, it was a matter of crossing Exeter Street and they would be at the rear of the theater.

Lydia set Sadie down behind her as she peered out from behind the aluminum-clad building to look at the street.

"There are only a few of them out there. If we time it right, we can make it across the street before they see us." She did not bother looking at Megan and Jason as she spoke. Lydia was the only one who could see the entire street from where they hid, but they could all hear what was going on out there.

Megan knew even from her tucked-down position behind Lydia that there wasn't a chance in hell they wouldn't be spotted.

The back door to the donut shop was locked. A layer of slick grease had leaked out from underneath it, all the way to the dumpster twenty feet back from the building. The coagulated oil and smell of spoiled butter coming from the shop tempted Megan. Despite its slight funk, the scent brought back memories of fresh baked goods. Her stomach, confused and rebellious, spoke its piece with an acidic gurgle. Megan's hunger had grown over the past few days to the point where she felt ravenous all the time. On top of that, the sun had sucked every last bit of moisture out of her body. At least the saliva created by the images of fried bits of glazed dough covered with icing allowed the gummy thickness in her mouth to loosen.

As Lydia watched the street, her eyes were drawn to an elderly man half a block away. He was digging through an overflowing trashcan that had fallen over on the sidewalk. Something must have crawled into it, perhaps a rat or even a cat, because the old man was doing a strange dance as he stooped over the opening. He would dig inside and then pull back, stumbling as he tried to regain his balance. To Lydia it looked as if he could barely stand—he was feeble and looked intoxicated. His slender legs added to the cartoonish image: two pipe cleaners propping up a slack body that looked warped, only a caricature of a human being. She dismissed him as she scanned the other stiff forms standing even closer to their position.

"I'm scared, Nanna Ly-Ly," Sadie cried out from behind her.

Lydia whipped around, alerted to the danger the child's voice represented. Sadie flung her little body at Lydia, wrapping her tiny arms around the grandmotherly figure.

"I don't want them to get us, Nanna!"

"Shh. Hush now, Sadie. Everything is going to be okay, but you have to keep quiet," Lydia whispered in Sadie's ear as she tried muffling the little girl's mouth in her ample bosom. She could feel the hot sting of tears on her t-shirt as the five year old wept.

Lydia nearly crushed Sadie in a desperate bear hug as she wrapped an arm around the child's face and clamped her hand over her mouth. But it was too late. Sadie's cries shattered the monotony of the moans on the street as they echoed between the buildings. Worse yet, the sound of her wretched sadness had been joined almost immediately by Joey and Nathan's sympathetic keening. There was almost relief in their cries, as if a steam pipe under tremendous pressure had burst, spewing out a hot blast of frustration that they had been feeling ever since the camp had come under attack.

Megan reacted as quickly as Lydia, her eyes first darting toward Sadie and then down at Joey, who clutched her hand with a frantic resolve. She knelt to comfort him but already sensed it was hopeless as Nathan chimed in. Gritting her teeth and clamping her hands on Joey's shoulders, Megan hushed and cooed at him, whispering plaintively for him to be quiet, the whole time knowing it was pointless and yet unable to think of anything else to do. Exasperated and fearful, she looked toward the street. That was when she saw the old man staring at them.

At the moment all he was doing was staring. More specifically, in the instant Megan looked in his direction, it appeared he was staring directly at her, right into her eyes. A mouse-like squeak escaped her throat.

Lydia was still desperately trying to silence Sadie when someone started shaking her shoulder. The frazzled woman tried to shrug the hand off, but felt fingernails digging into her skin. When she glanced up, Megan was pointing to the street with a terrified look in her eyes.

Standing, Lydia shivered as she scanned the road. The tension in her shoulders eased as she realized Megan's fear had stemmed from the few wrecked and twisted bodies heading in their direction. This was no advancing horde. It was several small groups of stiffs moving in to attack, spread wide across her field of vision. Lydia's eyes did not seek out the old man at the trashcan this time. He, like the other ghouls in the background, was a hazy shadow presenting no immediate threat.

In less than a heartbeat, she knew what she had to do. The children would continue to cry, and their path would only get more clogged the longer they waited. There were monsters on the street, yes, but they could make it to the theater if they kept low.

She glanced back at the others as she scooped up Sadie. "Follow me!"

Megan was stunned as she watched Lydia tear across the parking lot toward the street. The sixty year old dodged a small cluster of ghouls that had heard the cries of the children and moved in to investigate. The rotting creatures were surprised by the woman who burst out from behind the building, but reacted with the same ponderous and lethargic energy with which they did everything. They slowly turned and tottered after Lydia as she ran past them.

Megan glanced at Jason, motioning for him to follow. They gripped Joey and Nathan's hands and urged the boys to get moving. Tears still flowed, but the crying stopped as the quartet ran for the parking lot.

Lydia came to a sudden halt out on the road. The three ghouls she had passed in the parking lot were not the only ones that had spotted her. There were more stiffs on the street than she had estimated from the back of the donut shop, and an even greater number were pouring from every opening and gap between the buildings lining the roadway. The asphalt vibrated beneath her feet from the massive thrum of moaning voices, and everywhere she looked, there were more bodies coming toward her. Even the theater she hoped would provide sanctuary had several contorted human shapes oozing out of the shattered rear door.

Lydia barely heard Megan scream her name as panic overwhelmed her. Clutching Sadie close, she spun around in hopes of finding a gap in the thickening ranks of ghouls. It was only then that she noticed the old man who had been rooting through the trash can. From a distance, he had looked insignificant, a feeble old wreck.

But now he was standing directly in front of her.

Before she could react, his arm shot out and wrapped around the back of Lydia's head. The octogenarian let out a bloodcurdling scream as his jaw went wide. He bit deep into the side of her face, and a scream erupted from her throat. The teeth lodged in the muscles toward the back of her jaw, just below the ear. A freshet of blood burst free and splashed the cannibal as he braced his feet and moved his free arm to the opposite side of her face.

Megan and Jason avoided the same three slow-moving assailants in the parking lot with ease. One even tripped over its own feet, confused by the choice of targets. As the survivors kept moving out toward the street, Megan saw the old man running, actually running, toward Lydia. She screamed to warn her friend, but it was too late.

To Megan, it was as if he had glided up to Lydia, cutting a straight path at a speed not normally seen in the undead. As he closed in, she could see his eyes. They were huge floating pools of darkness that defied reason. The infected all had milky white eyes with barely visible pupils. Not this old man. His eyes were as dark as charcoal.

She watched in horror as Lydia was held in place by the old man's embrace. His head shook like a terrier with a rat caught between its teeth, and his victim nearly collapsed. She tried to sink to the ground, but his gripping claws held her up. Megan's own scream died, allowing her to hear the high-pitched screech coming from Lydia as the ghoul's teeth dug even deeper into the fibrous muscles of her jaw.

The next moment was a blur as Jason sped past Megan and jumped on the man's back, injured arm and all. Remarkably, Sadie had remained attached to Lydia during the attack—the child's arms still wrapped around her protector's shoulders. Jason's weight forced all of them to the ground as the ghoul's stiff legs collapsed under their combined weight.

Megan watched in horror as Jason fought to get a grip on the man's face, but his hand became slick as blood poured out of the jagged tear in Lydia's face. Megan could see a little leg sticking out of the pile and realized Sadie was stuck somewhere in the jumble of bodies.

Taking a step back, Megan felt the weight of Nathan and Joey pressing on her back. The boy's wailing mixed and mingled with the cries of the infected until it was impossible to tell the difference. She could see the same dark shadows Lydia had seen moments before as the cursed and condemned inched closer to her position. The rational part of her mind screamed for her to run, to just grab the boys and flee. They could find another hiding place if they left now. But Megan knew that her heart couldn't bear the loss of another friend ... not after having already lost everyone else about whom she had ever cared.

The howl of frustration that poured from her lips was raw and painful—a fair match to the cries all around her. Several cloudy eyes, which had been focused on the battle taking place nearby, rose up to look at her. For a moment, the infected thought they had heard a kindred spirit, but as they glared at Megan, they realized she was not one of them.

Staring at the bleeding pile of bodies, Megan's mind went blank, much like it had when she picked up that broken antenna and jammed it into that biker's eye. She moved forward, dragging the boys behind her.

As they approached the skirmish, she let Nathan and Joey go as she dug into the pile of bodies. With a strength that would have shocked her only moments before, she pushed Jason aside and snagged a handful of the ghoul's hair. She knew she only had one chance to do this right. Tightening her grip and giving a mighty yank, Megan heard the sickening sound of flesh and muscle tearing away from bone. The ghoul had already bitten through most of the muscle on Lydia's jaw, which made her job all the easier. Lydia tore free from her captor.

Without hesitation, Megan drove the ghoul's head into the pavement. There was some resistance, but with a mouth full of meat, the stiff was too preoccupied to fight back. There was a satisfying clunk as bone connected with the hard surface. Megan plowed her knee into the side of the vile creature's skull and punched at him wildly.

She could not recall how many blows she landed, but she didn't stop until the old man's movements ceased. As Megan relinquished her grip on the pulpy remains, she could feel an ache in her arm and a fire in her chest, but she had a clear understanding of what needed to be done.

"Grab Sadie! Move it!"

Jason looked dully at Megan as she dropped down beside Lydia and barked out the order. Lydia's long gray mane was damp with the blood running freely from her face. She made an ineffective attempt to cover the ragged wound with one hand, her fingers camouflaged in red.

"Jason!" Megan yelled. He nodded and moved toward Sadie, who was still latched onto Lydia's waist. Reaching down, Jason grabbed the little girl as he grimaced in pain. Despite using only his good arm to attack Lydia's assailant, his injured elbow had been batted around as well.

Sadie resisted at first and clung fiercely to Lydia, but as Megan helped the traumatized woman to her feet, the little girl relinquished her grip. Jason reached for her tiny hand and moved toward the boys. Nathan and Joey were statues, frozen in silence, but the twelve year old barely saw them as his eyes widened.

"MEGAN!"

Megan heard Jason's shout as she attempted to drape Lydia's hand over her shoulder.   When she looked over at him, her heart sank. They had forgotten about the three ghouls in the parking lot.

Two were already close to Jason, who had taken up a protective stance in front of the children. The third was still in the parking lot, having just climbed back to its feet after falling over earlier.

"No!" Megan screamed, running toward Jason and leaving Lydia behind. One of the two rotters, a sexless blob of rancid flesh, was taking a feeble swipe at the boy. The other, a woman in a pair of tight polyester pants and a bedazzled white blouse, heard Megan's scream and happily shifted her attention to the emaciated woman. Megan stopped short of the extended arms, but made sure she had the creature's undivided attention. It crept toward her as she inched back.

Jason easily dodged the other ghoul's weak attempt to grab him. He was grateful for Megan's quick intervention, but had no more idea of what to do than she did. He looked at the pathetic figure in front of him and gritted his teeth. It smelled ripe and gassy, the graying monster bloated to the point where its features made it look like a giant smiley face rather than an actual human being. Jason ducked another clumsy swipe and danced sideways.

Lydia, weak and fighting delirium, used her free hand to pull the children close. Her head spun as she fought to remain on her feet. She knew the youngsters were staring at the hand covering the mangled remains of her face, and she had no idea how to convince them everything would be okay. Sadie smiled at her, a gesture the mauled woman could not return. Even speaking was going to be difficult with her jaw in its current condition.

Lydia stumbled, feeling the world grow dark and cold around her. Her eyelids fluttered, but she managed to remain conscious as she saw Megan dart around some snarling woman in a tacky outfit. Jason was nearby, contending with some faceless monster taking ragged swipes at him. At the same time, a third ghoul was creeping up behind the other two, threatening to shift the odds in the infecteds' favor.

Lydia hissed a ragged sigh. The realization that her constant battle to survive was done calmed her. As the pain buzzed in her head and threatened to consume her, she resisted the urge to fall to the ground. Darkness threatened to consume her vision. She was growing dizzy from the loss of blood, but was coherent enough to know what needed to be done.

Out of the side of her face that was still working, she tried to speak to the children. The blood sloshing around in her mouth made her gag as she moved her throat muscles. It felt like a giant bag of salt mixed with alcohol had been poured into her open wound, and she leaned over to let the blood run down her face. Spitting was impossible. Ignoring the coppery taste, Lydia sucked in another breath. Her mouth was clear for a moment. She leaned over and looked down at the children. She hoped they could understand her garbled words.

Chapter 16

Lydia was a solidly built woman. "Thick," as her husband had once put it when he was a bit tipsy and couldn't stop his nearly fatal slip of the tongue. So when she plowed into the brittle figure and drove it backwards, there were several sickening snaps as its weakened bones broke under the pressure of the swift assault. She had angled her attack, intentionally or not, so that she took down both Megan's attacker and the third ghoul, spinning them sideways to the hardtop. The three crashed with a unified *whump!* Lydia's shredded mouth sprayed blood and gobs of loose flesh as she howled like an enraged banshee.

Jason was still busy dodging the troglodyte-like beast he was facing when he heard the scream, as did the warped blob of flesh in front of him. It paused, halting its persistent dance, and sniffed the air, though it was hard to understand how it could do so with such a swollen and cracked nose. Then it turned, Jason apparently forgotten. The boy froze, suspecting a trick even though he was certain the infected were incapable of deceit. When the slug moved away, he could only stare at its backside in complete shock.

Jason took a tentative step forward, fearing the bloated abomination that had attacked him was going after Megan. Instead, he saw movement a few feet to her left, and his eyes were drawn to a tangle of bodies writhing on the ground. That was where his adversary was headed. Megan's ghoul and the other that had been creeping up on her were in the pile with someone else covered in fresh blood. It hissed and howled as it dragged its nails across their putrefied flesh and attempted to bite at them despite its mangled jaw. The third ghoul fell into the pile, and the maddened creature reached out for it, excited to have another victim to obliterate.

Jason watched, motionless, as it dawned on him that it was Lydia in the pile. He went cold as he saw one of the creatures sink its teeth into her arm. She didn't seem to notice as she smashed her elbow into the throat of another. Her eyes were ablaze with anger as she ripped her arm free and tore off a gob of flesh from the face of another enemy. Blood sprayed from her arm, and she howled again, but not in pain.

Without realizing it, Jason moved toward the pile. An instant later, he felt someone pulling him away. Dazed, he looked back at Megan. She shook her head, fighting back tears.

"You can't do anything for her. We have to get out of here!"

The words didn't register, and he looked back at Lydia. She was still moving, twisting around as she landed a solid punch to the jaw of one of the creatures beneath her. Despite the damage from the tackle, the two original ghouls looked none the worse for wear, still moving and clawing at the homicidal woman as she beat on them. She doled out an equal share of punishment to the third, shifting away from its snapping teeth as she scratched at it. Her screams sent a shiver through Jason's heart as he saw another set of teeth sink deep into her shoulder. Another hand rose up out of the pile of loose body parts, and its fingers raked furrows across the now-exposed flesh of Lydia's back. The hand continued to dig into her flesh, scratching, burrowing as she writhed and tried to wriggle free.

"She's dead already, Jason. Please ..."

Jason stared at Lydia for a moment longer and then turned away, his own eyes stinging with tears as he reached for Megan. They turned to the children, and twin looks of surprise crossed their faces as they saw them standing there, a few feet away, holding hands. All three looked frightened, but Sadie, standing in the middle, looked almost tranquil, as if she had undergone some type of transformation.

Relieved, Megan gestured for the children to join them as they began to run.

She wondered how much time had elapsed since they had moved onto the street. It couldn't have been long, yet the little clump of breathers was now the center of attention for every slug within earshot. Megan knew there were hundreds more of them beyond sight range that knew exactly where they were. The cacophony, the roar of the dead, spread outward like ripples on a pond. More were coming. Many more.

Night would be upon them soon. The summer sun's harsh rays were subsiding, weakening and dimming as they fell beyond the horizon. The moving shapes progressed ever forward, casting long shadows on the street. These darkened outlines on the ground were distant specters reaching out for the survivors, closing the distance with elongated arms and fingers wriggling in anticipation.

Megan and Jason looked for cracks or breaks in the gathering crowd and saw none. There was nowhere to run. There were ebbs and flows to the oncoming tide of death, but none promising freedom. When a gap opened for an instant, it was immediately filled with more rotting bodies. Megan took a shuddering breath and looked back at the donut shop.

There was no hesitation as she took the only option remaining: they had to backtrack. Several apish shapes, bent over and dragging defective appendages, had passed in front of the curio shop next to Tom's and were coming for them. There wasn't much time.

"Behind the building. We can lose them back there and find another place to hide." The words came out breathlessly, but Jason understood.

Through the tinted windows of the donut shop, Megan could see several booths and a counter that ran half the length of the shop. A register stood to the left in front of the racks of empty donut displays. None of the windows had been shattered.

She looked back at her wards. Jason was holding Joey's

hand, and he was pulling the other two children along behind him like a little train. They were far enough away from Lydia that they could no longer hear her screams over the racket of the crowd. Shouts and cries reverberated off the windows of the donut shop, giving the unsettling impression that the ghouls were right next to them.

Megan turned back toward the donut shop and stopped dead. A keening noise spilled out of her lips as she saw that the narrow passage between the two buildings was now clogged with bodies. Several shadows moved toward them through the gap.

Jason saw them as well, and the rest of the little group skidded to a halt. The moving shadows between Tom's Donuts and the curio shop were taking shape, and he could see faces staring out at him. He could also see the milky whites of their eyes as they reflected the last of the sun's rays.

"Megan?"

Megan bit her lip to avoid screaming at Jason to leave her alone. Her head felt as though it was being squeezed by some massive force, and she was trembling with a terror beyond anything she had ever experienced before. They had perhaps a minute, maybe two, before the fiends inching closer tore them to pieces.

Taking a deep breath, Megan fought the faintness that threatened to overcome her and looked around once more. Each filthy and contusion-laced body she saw was worse than the last. They were everywhere. There were still pockets of open space on the street, but they were slowly being filled. She knew instinctively that even if they could manage to weave through those gaps, they wouldn't make it more than a hundred yards before being slaughtered.

Turning back toward the donut shop, she looked through the plate glass window. That was it. It was the only option left.

Pointing frantically at the building, she looked back at Jason and shouted at him. "Come on!"

Snatching up Nathan's hand, Megan did not wait for the kid's response as she ran for the entrance. The splinter of hope remaining in her gut felt like a blowtorch, burning away everything else as her feet pounded on the pavement.

She focused on the door's handle as they got close. Closing the last few feet, Megan reached out for it, her entire body quivering as she felt the cold metal beneath her fingers. Taking a deep breath, she tugged.

The door didn't budge.

Rattling it again, Megan slammed her fist against the glass, and still it did not move. She howled in frustration, beating on the door and cursing at it.

Jason reached out to her and touched her shoulder. Megan shook him off as she continued to slam her fist ineffectively against the door.

After a few moments, the boy spoke. "Megan, please. They're getting close. What do we do?"

Stopping the senseless pounding, Megan leaned her head against the glass and shuddered. She could hear the pleading in Jason's voice and the sound of the children crying. The sounds felt like drips of acid in her ears.

Turning away from the door, she wiped tears from her eyes, opened her arms, and pulled Sadie and the boys toward her. She felt the little bodies tremble as the three children latched on to her like a lifeline. Putting a hand around Jason's neck, she pulled him close as well.

Megan could see the question in his eyes and could barely stand the frantic hope remaining there. Jason was still counting on her to save them.

Her heart shattered as she shook her head and watched the boy's face crumble, the belief that they were somehow going to make it dying inside of him. Megan guided his head to her shoulder and hushed the children.

Taking one last glance out at the parking lot, she shivered. There, out where Lydia had fallen, was a countless mass of ghouls. They surrounded whatever remained of the gentle soul who had been caretaker of the children. That she was dead and no longer in pain gave Megan no relief as she watched the teeming mass of bodies push and pull at one other in an effort to collect a scrap of meat. The rest of the monstrosities had pushed past the bloody feast and were making their way toward the front of the donut shop. Catching her breath, Megan averted her eyes and stared down at the children huddled around her.

Moments later, there was a roar behind them, and they all tensed, squeezing as close to Megan as possible. It was a brief and sudden outburst that faded into the background of gibbering howls and crazed screams.

Bending her head, Megan pressed up against the children, cherishing their warmth and life as she prayed to God that the end would be quick and, if possible, painless ... at least for the children.

As she heard the steady beat of slogging feet and ruined bones dragging close, she whispered to the children, "Everyone, close your eyes."

Chapter 17

"Hey, babe."

Megan reached out to her husband with both hands, pressing against his shoulders, doing her best to push him back down. As she did, she noticed the silver revolver in her right hand.

"Don't try to get up, honey. You need to just lie there. You're dead."

Dalton smiled. It was a little disconcerting with a bullet hole winking at her from his forehead.

"Babe, I'm perfectly fine." He took her tiny hands in his much bigger ones as he got up.

"But I shot you."

Dalton sighed. "You don't get it, do you, Meg?"

He lifted one of his hands and rubbed at his eyes. Megan noticed how tired he looked.

God I miss him, she thought. It was a strange to think that. He was right here in front of her. So why was she missing him?

"Because I'm not actually here, Megan. I've been dead for a long time. You're just imagining me."

Megan's eyebrow arched as she gave her husband a skeptical look.

"What the hell are you talking about?"

Dalton smiled. "I know you want to forget everything that's gone on over the past few days, sweetie, but you can't."

Megan let out a hiss of angry breath. "What in the hell are

you talking about?"

"You know what I'm talking about. You just don't want to accept it."

Megan shook her head, baffled. "No, I think you don't know what's going on, and you're trying to confuse me for God knows what reason." Megan inched backwards as Dalton moved closer to her. After a heartbeat, she stopped.

Why am I afraid of him?

"Because of the dreams you've had about me since I've been gone."

Megan saw the sadness in his eyes.

"What ... what dreams are you talking about?"

Dalton looked uncomfortable, his feet shifting underneath him as he stared at the floor. "The ones where I come back to kill you."

*

They were sitting at the kitchen table. The space was light and airy, with the sliding back door that went down to their little patio behind them. Megan thought it was kind of strange that all the boards that had been put up to make sure the exit was secure were gone, but it was nice to look out on their back yard. The kitchen was nice and tidy, as was the family room. That was how she liked it, and she always did her best to keep up with the cleaning. But something was out of place.

"This is a dream."

Megan's head swiveled around toward her husband. The bullet hole was gone and he was in his old 'work around the yard' clothes. A ratty t-shirt and his baggy shorts with the paint stains on them. She stared at him, trying to take in the changes that had taken place in him since ... since they had been down in the basement.

How long ago was that?

"It was just a few seconds ago, sweetie."

"Stop doing that!"

Megan stood up, nearly knocking her chair over as she rushed to the kitchen. She made for the sink, her hands shaking as she grabbed a cup out of the strainer and held it under the spout. When she lifted it, nothing came out.

"There's no water, babe."

Dalton did not try to dodge the cup as it sailed toward his head. It bounced off his shoulder and rattled to the ground. He didn't even blink.

"What are you trying to do to me?" The words came out in a single blast of confusion and rage as Megan gesticulated frantically with her bird-thin arms. "What the hell is going on around here, Dalton? What's happening to me?"

Megan felt her legs weakening beneath her, and she slid to the floor.

"What am I doing here?"

Dalton walked over to her. "You are trying to block out what's happening to you. You don't want to think about it or feel it. So your mind just shut down, and tada! You were here, in the safest place you know."

Megan listened to the vague words and tried to understand what they meant. "Is that all you can tell me?" She couldn't keep the resentment out of her voice.

Dalton knelt down in front of her. She lifted her head and looked into his eyes. "But Megan, you already know all you need to know. You don't need me to tell you a thing."

She wanted to get angry, indignant. Throw out a scathing remark or yell at him. Anything to get him to give her a better answer. She didn't like playing these cutesy games with Dalton. But when she opened her mouth, nothing came out. She knew that he was right.

"Megan!"

The shouted word sent a ripple of shock through Megan's body.

"You can't stay here! You came here to escape the pain, but you have to go back, now!"

Dalton was standing, pulling her up with him. The sudden change in his demeanor was more than startling; it frightened her terribly.

"But I don't want to go back! I don't even know what I'm going back to, because you won't tell me!"

"Megan!"

Her husband shook her, rattling her teeth. She looked at him, not even sure who he was. Other faces swam before her eyes. A man who was not her husband, but someone for whom she cared a great deal ... a boy ... an African American boy with gentle eyes ... a little girl with long blond hair.

She broke free of her husband's grasp. Stepping backwards, she shook her head violently. "No. No, no, no. I DON'T WANT TO GO BACK!"

Dalton didn't move. "They need you, Megan. You have to go back."

"But I want to stay here with you!"

He was already starting to fade. His voice was a whisper as she watched his eyes. She could see the rest of the kitchen and the table behind him, but they weren't much more substantial than he was.

"Remember, my love, this is just a dream. You can only dream for so long, and then you have to wake up."

Megan closed her eyes, and she could see it all. The children, Jason, the monsters coming for them. They were there, suffering alongside her. Waiting to die. Looking to her for a little comfort while they still lived. Just a few moments of pain, and it would all be over.

She opened her eyes. Dalton stood right in front of her, his face only a few inches away from hers, his eyes wide open. The bullet wound in his forehead had reappeared. Her heart stopped.

"MEGAN!" he shouted at her.

She began to scream.

*

"Megan!"

She kept her eyes shut, her heart racing as she bit down on the scream. She was huddled with the children crammed between her, Jason, and the glass wall of the donut shop. The noise surrounding her was so loud that it felt like another wall closing in, pressing up against her back. Swimming through that noise were clammy claws, coming to rip her away from those she was trying to protect, claws that would pull her out into the crowd. She wondered if she would manage to keep her eyes closed as rotten teeth sank into on the flesh of her arms, legs, breasts. Perhaps, if she was lucky, the bellows from dead throats saturated with her blood and bits of meat might drown out the last sounds of the children as they were torn apart alongside her.

"Megan!"

She closed her eyes tighter, and she wanted to cover her ears, but could feel Jason twisting away from her. She tried to get a grip on him, but he freed himself. Megan whimpered but still refused to open her eyes as she held onto the other children.

She felt a hand on her shoulder a few seconds later, and she almost screamed as she was pulled around. Opening her eyes was almost an involuntary reflex. It was Jason, standing in front of her and pointing, his eyes filled with excitement.

"MEGAN, God dammit! Please!"

It wasn't Jason speaking. He was already gawking at the sea of bodies milling around them. Megan didn't want to do the same, but she forced her eyes to stay open.

All her nightmares were arrayed before her; it was like a single organism made up of everyone who had ever been consumed by the super-virus. Appendages swayed and flapped like tentacles writhing on some dark beast out of the abyss, hypnotically gesturing for Megan to join them in their agony. It tasted the air, seeking out warm flesh. It would not just consume her and the children—it would absorb them so they could become one with it. Her chest shuddered as she took the graveyard air into her lungs and looked out at the monstrous legion arrayed against them. The shock to her system came not only from the infected in front of her, though it was obliterating in its potency, but from realizing that while they flowed and rippled all around her, their animosity and their ferocity were directed not just at her, but in several different directions.

"Ben?"

Megan did not hear the tentative word that spilled from Jason's lips, but watched in amazement as the behemoth of a man burst through a tightly knit crowd of ghouls nearby.

They were debris before him, dried-out autumn leaves that crunched and crumbled as he bellowed in rage and slapped them out of the way. His voice overwhelmed all the keening and crying that surrounded him.

It dawned on Megan that his voice was the noise she had heard before—the roar she believed was the sound of the mob closing in on them. It was, in fact, the angry bellow of the man currently barreling into three persistent attackers. As they fell to the ground, Ben stomped on the revenants, using his mass to crush their skulls beneath his giant boot heel.

"MEGAN!"

Her head whipped around as she heard her name once again. Megan felt dizzy and feared it was just her mind playing tricks, as it had to be with Ben. Then she saw something: a shape gliding quickly through the crowd. Her eyes darted back and forth, trying to catch another glimpse as she clung to the children.

"Megan, over here!"

Megan's world froze as her eyes found the spot from which the voice came. A clash of emotions, of agony and euphoria, spilled over her as she saw a face above the crowd, somehow floating above everyone else. It was a face she knew well.

It was Jeff.

Time snapped back into place as Jason grabbed her by the arm and spun her around. "It's Ben! It's Ben!" He was trying to straighten out his lame arm and point as he hopped up and down. Megan nodded, but she did not turn, fearful that Jeff would dissolve, reveal himself as a figment of her imagination if she broke eye contact with him.

Jason was confused by how unimpressed Megan was at the startling news. But as he followed her eyes, his knees nearly gave out. Instead, he pumped his fist and whooped in delight.

His excitement convinced Megan that Jeff was no mirage. He was still there, standing on top of a station wagon, swinging a long metal pole above his head and trying to get her attention. He was above the crowd, across the street.

Megan waved as Jason continued to holler in celebration. The cheer was cut off as they saw the metal pole come crashing down on a woman's head. She had been trying to crawl on top of the Taurus to get at Jeff, but now slumped back to the ground.

Megan kept her eyes focused on Jeff while Jason looked back and forth between the two men. A cold revelation gripped her: their friends were trying to save her and the children, but were committing suicide to do so. The station wagon on which Jeff stood would be completely surrounded soon. She moved away from the safety of the donut shop toward him, letting go of the small hands wrapped in her own without even realizing it, until Jason grabbed her arm, pulling her back. Megan glared in anger at him until she saw the look of fear on his face. She looked down at the children and realized what she had been about to do.

They stood and watched, helpless, as the two madmen kept the crowd's attention. Ben picked up a police officer and raised him, squirming, over his head. He had the ghoul by the throat and crotch, and the giant was not straining a bit as he launched the cop, flailing limbs and all, into a group of five incoming stiffs that had made the mistake of being clumped too close together. Still, more of the squirming forms in the street were coming for Ben.

The same could be said for Jeff, who jumped off the car and ran screaming like a wild man as a wake of corrupt bodies followed. He shifted gears and turned sharply to avoid another group, swinging his oversized weapon at a man wearing the remains of a three-piece suit. The blow was only glancing, flattening the businessman's partially detached ear, but it was enough to allow Jeff to get by. He ran, sliding through clusters of agitated bodies reaching out for him.

Megan grimaced as she saw that there were still small pockets of rotters not taking the bait and ignoring the two men. Some were starting to notice the quiet group huddled against the wall again.

"They're still coming for us."

Jason forced his eyes away from Ben and tracked the rest of

the crowd. At least a couple dozen ghouls would be on top of them in less than a minute if they didn't get moving soon.

As he continued to stare at the crowd, Megan felt the tug of a small hand on her arm. She didn't want to look away from the hypnotic advance of bodies; she tried to ignore the sensation, but it was persistent. She looked down to see Sadie's big round eyes staring up at her.

"Is Ben going to save us?"

Megan's heart was already shattered into a hundred pieces, but the desperate plea crushed her even more. Sadie tried waving at Ben, but it came as no surprise that the man did not see her. Nathan and Joey were catatonic with fear while the little girl seemed very aware of what was happening.

Jason heard the question and turned to Megan, who could feel the weight of both sets of eyes waiting for her answer. She opened her mouth, trying to force something out, but she could find no words. Taking a shuddering breath, Megan tried to see where Jeff had gone, but she couldn't spot him.

"Megan, Jason! This way!"

Megan wanted to scream in surprise at the new voice coming from her left, near Ben, but she had nothing remaining inside that would allow her to do so. Almost as if she had no will of her own, she turned in the direction of the voice.

It was George. Of course it was George. Jason was already moving toward the man, dragging Nathan, who followed like a robot. The boy moved his feet, but his stunned face showed no reaction to the potential rescue. George was at the corner of the building, in the gap between the donut and curio shops, waving them forward. Ben had moved the crowd far enough away from the strip of asphalt between the two buildings that the little group of survivors could squirm through.

Megan felt nauseated as she moved, grabbing Joey and Sadie's hands and pulling them beside her at a half run. She understood now: Ben and Jeff were the bait so George could get them out of there. Her eyes remained focused on him as her heart flooded with guilt at the thought of the other two men's sacrifice.

George was drenched with sweat, and his shirt was ripped, but he looked okay. He was toting another large piece of wood. It looked cracked and abused, ready to shatter, but menacing all the same.

Jason crashed into George, hugging him with his good arm. The big man's expression changed to relief as he returned the affectionate embrace. There was a smile on his face as he looked past the boy to Megan. For a moment, the smile faltered as the two adults shared a brief, sad moment.

They both understood. As Megan came trotting up, there was no need for words. Whatever regrets either of them had needed to be put aside. They could pray for the survival of the other two men later. For now, all they could concern themselves with was making their escape from this deathtrap.

They moved around the corner toward the rear of the shop. They were only a few seconds ahead of the advancing horde.

Chapter 18

The small group of survivors disappeared from view. Several of the rigor-riddled forms that had been advancing toward them when they were stationary immediately lost interest and shifted their attention to Ben, who was not too far away and didn't seem interested in fleeing. His scent was far too tantalizing to resist.

Most of the revenants broke off their pursuit of Megan and the others, but a few continued moving toward the gap between the buildings. The one leading the way was not as stiff limbed, though she was just as maimed as the others. Her wounds were fresh. A spray of blood from the shredded muscles in her legs, arms, and face served as a bright decoration on her torn clothing.

The gray-haired woman tried to moan through a broken and dangling jaw. A bubbling hiss was all that came up from her throat, but it was enough to attract several other ghouls nearby. She had the scent of the children on her. It was a rich, sweet aroma that excited them as they followed her between the buildings toward their prey.

Chapter 19

Jeff took a frantic swing at a stiff-necked farmer standing in front of him. Solitary ghouls that interrupted his movements were becoming less the norm. The pole sent its vibrating message of agony down his arms as it connected solidly with the left side of the man's head and sent him staggering. It gave Jeff the moment he needed to slide past.

The gaps in the crowd were shrinking. Everywhere there were islands of moving shapes. Two or three clumped together, forcing him to barrel through them with the hope that his diminishing speed and power would prove sufficient to force his way to the next vacant spot. As he moved, so did the crowd, contorting and twisting to block his progress.

***

He was still trying to figure out how he had gotten here. When Ben found him and George, pulling them out of the sticky mess they had gotten themselves into near the cracked-up Mercedes, there had been little time for greetings. Ben had breathlessly told them that he thought he knew where the others were, and they were off and running.

They were amazed as he took them on a twisting route that avoided nearly all of the lumps of infected bodies. He picked his way around the town, slipping into various buildings and popping out onto other streets that were clear of traffic. All the while, the noise grew greater as they got closer to where their guide thought Megan and the children might be. Ben knew the town like the back of his hand and had been trying to track everyone's movements almost since the moment he had left the RV. He confirmed that Frank was dead and was able to guess Michael's fate as well. When they asked about Cindy, he had no answers, which made them move even faster.

When they finally spotted the others, it was already too late for Lydia. The three men watched from their hiding place across the street, shell shocked, as a crowd of undead tore her to pieces.

There was no time to mourn her death when they saw the rest of the group standing against the wall of the donut shop. Ben made the quick decision that George would guide Megan and the children to safety while he and Jeff would lure the mob away from them.

When George tried to protest, Ben bluntly stated, "You have a family out there. If you ever want to see them again, I suggest you shut the fuck up and do as I say."

That ended the argument before it even began.

Jeff remembered clasping hands with George moments later as he prepared to exit the building behind Ben, who had torn across the street, whooping and hollering like a lunatic.

"Take good care of them, okay?"

Before George could respond to the request, Jeff turned, rushing out of the building in Ben's wake. The metal post he was carrying whistled through the air and came down on the skull of the first ghoul he came across.

***

Jeff glanced around, his head on a pivot. Distant doorways beckoned. They teased and tempted him, but might as well have been a thousand miles away for all the hazardous terrain he would have to cross to get to them. A sudden wave of panic came and went as he lost sight of George and the others. Fighting to remain focused on his own problems, Jeff hoped that the little group had escaped the mess surrounding him and Ben as he dodged another grasping hand.

Something grazed his back, and he nearly jumped out of his skin. The claw that nearly scratched him snagged on the drenched material, ripping it. The burst of speed occasioned by the close call had the desperate survivor huffing as he moved down the road. He faked left and then squirmed between two crashed cars in the middle of the street, leaving a couple of stiffs wrestling with one another to be the first through the narrow gap.

Jeff stopped abruptly as he was greeted by a wall of ghouls on the other side of the cars. He resisted the temptation to jump on top of one of the cars as they closed on his position in a rough semicircle. The population on the street was reaching critical mass. If he climbed up on a car now, he would be surrounded in seconds.

He backed up involuntarily as the sounds of excited hunters closed from all directions. He tried to differentiate the sounds in back from those up front, but it was impossible. Noise blasted his eardrums from all directions. Looking behind, he saw three people clawing their way on top of the cars. The narrow gap between the vehicles had several of the sickly figures slicing themselves to ribbons trying to force their way through.

The impulse to jump on to the hood of the Hyundai and kick the riffraff away was tempting. A woman scratching at the edge of the front quarter panel was trying to gain purchase to pull herself up, though her eyes were glued to Jeff. All she could do was waddle and bounce pathetically off the side of the car. There were others behind, pressing up against her. Soon they would be able to get up and over the minor obstacle the cars presented. Turning back was not an option.

Jeff pressed his back up against the car, staring forward. They were coming from all sides; his peripheral vision confirmed that there were no gaps in the first layer of pusbags. As he scanned the crush of bodies in front of him, he let out a hot hiss of air as his shoulders slumped. There was nowhere left to turn, no niche to slip into and escape.

He closed his eyes. Just long enough to try to calm down, to block out the noise around him. Running was suicide, pure and simple, but he had no choice.

"Ben! I'm coming for you, man!" he screamed.

As he rushed forward, expending the last of his energy, there was no time to look at the small crowd of withered figures he bowled over to see if they were surprised by his assault. Whether they were caught off guard or not, Ben was a good fifty feet away, and the bodies were thick between him and the other man.

Jeff ran the gauntlet of cold, numb hands reaching out to grab him. He lowered his shoulder, smashing into them. He heard a roar from Ben that sent a shiver through his body as he pushed himself past what he thought he could endure, his legs pumping as he bashed through stiff carcasses like bowling pins. As the withered forms spun and fell away, Jeff clenched his teeth, throwing himself into another wave.

He cried out Ben's name again and saw him up ahead, looming over the crowd. It looked like he could almost reach out and touch the tall man, but there was still too much distance between them. Jeff's feet felt like they were stuck in wet cement, and his arms were numb from crashing into body after body. The frantic tangles of arms and torsos through which he had ripped moments earlier were not parting so easily anymore.

As he slowed, arms attempted to encircle him in a harsh embrace. He continued to struggle, shaking them off and pushing them away, avoiding the snapping teeth and desperate hunger. He couldn't move closer to Ben and was forced to duck and stab blindly with the corrugated pipe he still held in his bruised and weakened hands. There was a wet crunch as it slid between the ribs of a girl wearing a bloodstained bathing suit. The assault knocked her back, but ripped the weapon free from Jeff's hands as the metal shaft impaled her.

He threw an awkward punch, his fist crashing into the forehead of a stooped figure whose chest cavity was missing. The blow made the diseased fiend wobble backward. Jeff lashed out again, anger the only thing keeping him upright. The bodies pressed around him, hissing and moaning, reaching for his living flesh.

*****

Ben had heard Jeff yelling over the crackle of voices and tensed as he spotted him in the crowd. He marked his position as he moved, charging like a bull elephant through the crowd, knocking bodies aside like blades of grass. Jeff had been moving in his direction, but had slowed to a halt. It was clear his strength was depleted. Ben surged ahead, increasing his speed as he crushed bodies beneath his boots. He could feel claws scratching and teeth tearing at his clothing and did his best to ignore them as he plowed his way to Jeff. Five sets of hands vied to be first to grab hold of the man. He fought them off, though his blows were getting weaker by the second. Ben burst through the group and wrapped an arm around Jeff's midsection. A loud *oomph* greeted him as he drove his body upward, elevating the smaller survivor and shredding the hands tugging on him. With speed that had the stiffs swiping air, Ben pivoted, returning in the direction from which he had come.

Breaking free of the mob, he caused several ghouls to stumble and collapse to the ground, further slowing the pursuit. The crowd was now behind them, and after a minute of full-tilt speed, Ben was feeling the ache of carrying Jeff over his shoulder.

"Can you walk?"

Ben took the grunted response as a "yes" and unceremoniously dumped Jeff on the ground. He wore a look of confusion on his face.

"What the hell is going on?" Jeff demanded.

He was disoriented and weak, stumbling as he tried to keep his wobbly legs beneath him. And yet, there was a fire in his eyes that told Ben he wasn't ready to give up just yet.

"We're going after the others."

Testing his legs, Jeff discovered he could still walk. At least when there wasn't a crowd surrounding him, ready to tear him apart.

As they sped around the corner of a building, Jeff could hear both pursuit behind them and howling cries up ahead. The relief at being saved again by Ben disintegrated as he realized that they weren't out of danger and neither were the others.

"How many of those things were chasing them?"

Ben didn't bother looking at Jeff. He fought to keep the emotion off his face, but Jeff could see the concern there. They picked up speed, putting more distance between them and the pulsating mass of bodies back at the donut shop.

As the howls to their rear faded, Jeff's ears picked up noises ahead more clearly. They overrode his own heavy breathing as the pain in his legs and chest diminished. His friends were up ahead, somewhere, possibly dying already. The two men continued to run, dreading what they might see around the next corner, but still moving as fast as they could.

Their frightful thoughts were shattered as they heard an ear-piercing scream up ahead.

Chapter 20

Jeff sped up, passing Ben.   As he got closer, his heart pounding hard inside his chest, he had to stop short, his mouth agape and his eyes trying to register the scene in front of him.

There were only two words to describe it: utter chaos. George was grappling with a ghoul while two others attempted to join in the action, snatching at him, grabbing at his clothing. He still had the large piece of wood and was using it to push them back, with only minor success. Jason was next to him, swinging his good arm erratically in a wide circle. He lashed out with his feet as well, kicking and screaming, panic and rage taking over as five more ratty figures closed on him. More were behind them, a widely spaced group of perhaps eight to ten stiffs. But it was not the man and boy on whom Jeff had his eyes. Instead it was the other group of survivors only a few feet from where he stood.

It was almost too much to bear looking at. Nathan and Joey were on the ground, having been dragged down and swarmed over. Nathan, the boy with flaming red hair, was screaming as two ghouls played tug of war with him. They were not only pulling on his arms, but had already devoured several of his fingers. There was a sickening pop as his left arm jittered and the flesh ripped free. Jeff could see the arm tearing from the socket, the white bone barely visible before a geyser of blood spurted out, saturating the woman who somehow had the strength to pull the child's arm off. She slumped to the ground, satisfied with the small morsel while the other fiend, a teenage boy, continued his feast on the boy's other arm, working his way closer to Nathan's scrawny body. As for the boy, the screaming stopped as he choked on the torrent of vomit coming out of his mouth.

Joey had fared no better, though he had only one attacker. The naked, sexless ghoul had one arm wrapped protectively around the sandy-haired boy's neck as it gnawed on the skin above his ribcage. The other hand had found Joey's guts, ripping straight through the button-down shirt he was wearing and was knuckle-deep in the child's abdominal cavity. Joey's shirt and jeans were so saturated with blood that it was hard to guess what color they were. His face, thankfully, was slack, eyes open but staring straight up, arms flat at his sides. Joey was in shock, his mind shut down from the unbearable pain. Jeff blinked away the sting of tears as the monster on top of the innocent child wrenched several dark tube-like objects free from his abdomen.

Jeff's eyes were on the two boys for an instant, but as he ran up, he searched for someone else. When he spotted Megan nearby, he felt all the heat go out of his body. It took a few moments to comprehend what was happening. She was there, on the ground, her slight frame contorted as she wrestled with some blood-soaked harpy that was ignoring her. The gray-haired creature had its back to Jeff and appeared to have its arms wrapped around something tiny. For a wild moment, as he stumbled closer, he thought it was a puppy or kitten. The lunatic image passed as he inched forward, watching Megan ineffectually smash her fists against the woman as she screamed. It was not clear at first, but then he realized that Megan was not just screaming, she was speaking to the ghoul, repeating several words over and over again. Jeff's vision swam, and he felt faint when he realized what the monster was holding, cradled gently in its arms. At the same time he understood what Megan was saying.

He didn't hear Ben cry out from behind him or feel the slight breeze as the bulldozer of a man flew past, charging into battle. The weakened tendrils of Jeff's sanity that had been fraying all day were ready to snap. Megan was not weakly beating on just any ghoul; she was wrestling with Lydia, who appeared to have Sadie wrapped in a loving embrace. Megan screamed the woman's name, pleaded with her, begged Lydia to let Sadie go. But the disfigured woman was too busy trying to bite down on the girl's skull with her shattered jaw as the tiny blond girl screamed and thrashed within her grasp.

Megan's head whipped around and she replaced Lydia's name with Jeff's, pleading for him to do something, anything to save Mary ... because it was Mary, his baby girl, in the monster's grasp, not Sadie. She hadn't died back in his house, she was here, still alive. Frankie, his son, was just a few feet away, his intestines being ripped from his body. The woman screaming at him was no longer Megan, but Ellen, his wife, pleading with him.

"Are you going to let her die all over again? Are you going to let all of us die?"

"No," was all Jeff could whisper as he rushed forward.

*

Megan felt a hand grip her arm and yank her out of the way. She gave a surprised yelp as she tripped over her feet and fell on her ass. Jeff had almost pulled her arm out of its socket in his rush to get at Lydia.

Jeff latched onto the gore-stained mop of Lydia's hair and yanked her head back violently. There was a gurgling sound and a stream of tainted blood shot out of the woman's throat and sprayed Sadie. Lydia's skull was wrenched all the way to her backbone. Without missing a beat, Jeff grasped her loose jawbone and tore it free from its moorings. Megan, too stunned to turn away, watched as the remnants of Lydia's tongue squirmed and wriggled like a writhing snake in the open air. Before Lydia could relinquish her grasp of Sadie to deal with this new distraction, Jeff slammed the edge of the jawbone into one of her eye sockets. It was not a swift effort, but calm and precise. A single arm came up and pawed at him. Jeff swatted it aside and maneuvered the edge of the bone through the socket, rupturing the orb as he worked it around, twisting and digging. Megan's gorge rose as she heard a muffled pop, and Jeff's hand jittered as the bone slid past whatever resistance there was and moved into Lydia's brain. As he continued digging with the improvised weapon, the ghoul's arm convulsed. Lydia twitched one last time, and Megan gave in to the urge to vomit.

Jeff released his grip on Lydia's bloody mane and let the woman who had cut his hair that morning drop, boneless, to the ground. He could barely hear Sadie crying or the loud chewing noises going on directly behind him. The echoes of George and Ben's battle a few feet away did not register either as he turned his attention to the other ghouls.

There Frankie lay, on the dirty ground, his eyes staring blankly as the ghoul on top of him dug around in the child's abdomen and shoved handfuls of dark muck into its mouth. The smell of viscera was thick in the air as Jeff approached.

The monster did not notice the man standing behind it. It was far too engrossed in its meal to pay attention. Even when the hand landed on top of its head, it didn't react.

*

Megan gave her mouth a rough swipe with the back of her hand. She crawled over to Sadie, hoping against hope that the girl was still alive. Lydia had only taken hold of the child for a few seconds, but that was more than enough for the damage to be done. She shoved away the horrifying image of Jeff jamming the jawbone into Lydia's eye and his cold, distant expression as he did so. Instead, she focused on the little girl slumped on the ground next to the corpse of the woman she had considered a friend, though she barely knew her.

Megan gagged once more, fighting the desire to dry heave at the smell of fresh death surrounding her. She saw Ben, George, and Jason moving, twisting, and fighting several yards away, but she ignored them as well. All that mattered was Sadie.

She could hear the little girl whimpering. There was some relief at that. She was still alive. But if Lydia had bitten or scratched her … Megan trembled as she got close enough to look down at the girl.

"Goodbye, Nanna Ly-Ly. I love you."

Megan felt the sting of tears at the quiet words and saw Sadie, stained with dirt and darker substances, gently holding Lydia's hand to her cheek. The child did not see a monster, but the caring and selfless woman whom she loved dearly.

Megan felt as though she were hanging on by the thinnest of threads. Lydia was dead, Teddy was dead, and poor little Nathan and Joey … but Sadie was still alive, and she latched desperately onto that fact to keep from losing her mind.

She opened her arms to the little girl when Sadie looked up. She came to Megan, and her warm body pressed up against the frail woman. Closing her eyes, Megan let her tears mingle with Sadie's. With all the blood and muck covering the girl, it was hard to tell but she thought the child was okay. Lydia hadn't managed to bite her with her mangled jaw.

As she held her close, Megan heard a low keening noise rising up somewhere nearby. Only after she started shaking uncontrollably and found it hard to breathe did she realize the noise was coming from her own throat.

*

Jeff made quick work of the androgynous eating machine that had attacked Joey, driving his thumbs through its ocular cavities as he gripped its face. The wet mush that squirted out around his fingers was cold and runny, but he persisted, driving the tips of his thumbs into the rotten brain behind them. He was forced to slap away a hand that came up once or twice, but his task took only moments. Then it was time to move on to the next ghoul.

He advanced on the two ghouls ravaging Nathan. They were both busy feasting on various parts of the boy, their faces smeared with his blood. The pulped mess bore little resemblance to the redheaded kid anymore. One of the attackers had pulled the boy's upper lip until the nose and the flesh around both eyes were ripped free, leaving only the gleam of bare bone behind.

The heel of Jeff's hiking boot crashed down on the back of the female's head. Her skin had a greenish tint, and as she lurched forward he could see it blacken where his foot slammed into it. She didn't drop the arm on which she was gnawing, though most of the meat from the small bicep was already gone. The repugnant beast was focused on a rubbery piece of tendon still attached to the bone. As she looked back at her assailant, the vile creature hissed, aggravated and yet aroused by the interruption. She discarded Nathan's arm and tried to turn over, reaching for the fresh meat standing before her.

Jeff drove his knee into the woman's back, slamming her to the pavement. Her head rocketed off the hard ground, and a sound like a wet fart escaped from her midsection. A sewer-like stench hinted that her stomach had burst from the blow, and a moment later, the perforated organ spilled its vile, undigested contents onto the ground all around her.

The damage went unnoticed by the woman as she twisted and contorted in an effort to face Jeff. Wasting no time, he grabbed her ears and rammed her face into the pavement. He didn't stop until half her skull disintegrated and the bone and gooey flesh formed a stew-like mixture on the pavement around the remains of her head.

Not troubling to wipe the filth from his hands, Jeff stood up. His eyes locked on the teenage boy who had assisted the woman in Nathan's demise, his last victim already a faint memory.

The second revenant had his face buried in Nathan's abdomen, no longer bothering to use his hand to scrape out piles of stringy goo. He was a pig at the trough, rooting around in the bloody mess. Jeff looked beyond the teen at the remnants of Nathan's face. He did not see the bare bone on display. Instead, he saw the face of his own son again—skull smashed in by Jeff's own baseball bat. There was simply no denying that he was Jeff's boy, with the same dark hair, same brown eyes, same nose ...

The tears came as he slammed his booted foot down on top of the teenager's exposed neck. There was a sound like cracking knuckles—a sharp, crisp noise. Jeff put all his weight behind the blow and cringed as the teen's face was buried even deeper in Nathan's belly.

He felt faint and almost fell back as the teen resisted. Jeff's intention was to hold him down and pin him to the ground. But even after putting his full weight on the creature's neck and snapping the bones beneath his foot, there was still some fight left in the ghoul.

"I'm tired. I'm just so ... tired." He shook his head. "I can't do this anymore ... I-"

Jeff stumbled back and tripped over his own sluggish feet. He felt weak, disoriented. As he slammed into the pavement, the flash of pain that flared through his back jolted him, and he bit down hard on his tongue. As his mouth filled with blood and his eyes blurred with tears, he wailed in despair at the loss of his family.

As he curled into a ball and wept, Jeff didn't see George and the others watching him.

*

He jumped when Ben put a hand on his shoulder. It was a gentle gesture accompanied by a slight squeeze. The big man had already finished the job Jeff had started of dispatching the teen, while George and Jason tended to Megan and Sadie. Ben helped Jeff to his feet and made sure he could stand. The nearly broken man's wailing had ended, and while he seemed withdrawn, Jeff was able to stay on his feet as he stared down at Joey and Nathan's mangled bodies.

Ben's arrival had helped George make quick work of the stiffs they had been facing, his knife and George's two by four cutting them down quickly. When they'd turned to help Jeff, they, along with Jason, were horrified to see what had happened to Nathan and Joey, but were even more shocked to see the way Jeff was grimly dealing with the creatures that had mauled the children. When they realized Lydia was one of the obscenities he had executed, they were stunned beyond words.

George looked over at Ben, his eyes stricken. Ben's face had lost its confident aura. Their savior looked just as scared and shattered as the rest of them, as if all of this were too much to take. Ben had already backed away from Jeff, as if he were afraid to stay close to him for very long.

Megan, still clutching Sadie, fell into George's arms. After a few seconds, he gave her a quick squeeze and left her with Jason, who touched her and Sadie in turn, still finding it hard to believe they had made it. The twelve year old wrapped his arm around Megan and held the two females close. George moved to Ben to talk privately with him.

"What do we do now?" he whispered as he looked around the area. The bodies had piled up, and while they'd done away with the ghouls in the immediate area, it probably wouldn't take long before the crowd from the donut shop tracked them down. Distant moans and screams left no doubt that there were other infected on the march, coming for them from all over town. They probably had only a few minutes before they were swimming in the undead once again.

George could see the beads of sweat on Ben's brow and the sad, faint look of despair in his eyes. Despite everything the warrior had done to keep as many of them alive as possible, it was clear he wasn't feeling like much of a hero.

After taking a few moments to compose himself, Ben spoke. "We can go about two blocks down and hole up for a bit in a building I know is safe." He glanced at Jeff and then Megan before moving closer to George and speaking in a hushed voice. "Do you think the others will be okay?"

"I'm fine," Megan blurted out, her head popping up from where it had been buried in Jason's shoulder. She looked at Ben, her face drawn but those luminescent blue eyes of hers still coherent and clear as she spoke. Her jaw was set, and while she looked like hell, he could sense that the quietly resolute woman had not bottomed out quite yet. She shifted Sadie to her other shoulder as he nodded at her.

"Well then, I guess we better get moving," he said as he looked back at George.

"They're going to get back up."

Ben's back stiffened as he turned to Jeff. Everyone else's eyes were drawn to the haggard man as well.

"They always do."

The words were haunted, full of despair. Ben couldn't think of a response, and apparently George couldn't either. The two men stood side by side, like statues, as Jeff gazed down at the two boys.

"We need to take care of them." Though Jeff's words were full of desolation, they were steady. "We can't let them get back up."

Megan's face was a mask of horror as she tried to remove Sadie's clinging hands.

"No!" The word echoed around them, much louder than Jeff's whispered statement. All eyes were on Megan as she managed to free herself from the little girl and walked toward Jeff. "We can't do that to them! Are you insane?"

No one else spoke as she moved in on Jeff. "I am not going to let you ... do whatever it is you want to do to those poor children." She reached out and shoved him as her voice became a high-pitched squeal. "They're already dead, Jeff! What more do you want from them?"

She launched herself at Jeff, slapping and beating at him. He did nothing to avoid the blows as she continued screaming.

"Enough!" The deep voice startled Megan, and she turned to look at Ben. "We have to get out of here. Now! We don't have time for this bickering. Not if you want to live!"

"Ben, we can't do this to them. They've already endured so much pain ..." She fell into Ben's arms and pressed her face against his chest. A few seconds later, she pounded on him with her tiny fists. "It isn't fair! This isn't how it's supposed to be!"

Picking Megan up, Ben turned to face Jeff. She squirmed in his massive arms for a few seconds and then settled. There was little she could do to fight the big man, and she was far too tired to keep trying.

"I'm sorry." Jeff reached out to touch her. She cringed away from him at first, but as he reached for her again and continued speaking, Megan stopped resisting. He looked up at the darkening sky and shook his head, his breathing slow and labored. "I wish I could have said that to my wife and kids before they died ... that I was sorry."

Megan turned to look at him, confused. Jeff had never mentioned his wife or family before. Curiosity overrode her anger as she waited for him to continue.

"I would have told them how sorry I was for the things I did, the mistakes I've made." His eyes closed tightly as he punched at his leg repeatedly. "I'm sorry I left them alone. I'm sorry ... I'm sorry I screwed up." Jeff's eyes popped open. The look on Megan's face reflected the horror he felt.

"I killed my wife and children, Megan."

Her eyes widened as she shook her head in disbelief. She didn't understand.

"I left them. God! I can't believe I left them to go out and find food and water. But we were starving. It had been six fucking weeks! I counted the days on the calendar. Everyone else had turned into those things. All of our neighbors, everyone we knew. I didn't know what else to do.

"We were trapped in there. All that god-awful time. My daughter was a basket case. Ellen ... she was the one holding us together." A quivering smile crossed his lips. "She always was the strong one. It was deep down ... something you couldn't always see, but it was there. She knew how to calm Mary down, even when she couldn't stand the screams anymore. God, the screams ... the moans. It was driving us mad.

"My son ... he was only five for Christ's sake! How do you keep a five year old from going completely nuts under those circumstances? All he wanted to do was to help his dad. That's all! Mary was inconsolable. She was almost catatonic. Ellen couldn't watch the both of them, and I knew it. But I still left ... just so I could go find some goddamned food."

Ben let go of Megan, and she stood there, eyes wide as she watched Jeff tell his story. The others stared at him as well, adults and children alike. They were all mesmerized.

"When I came back, the door was unlocked. I knew I had locked it; I was sure I did. But it was unlocked ... and there was blood on it."

Jeff's distant eyes grew hard, and his back stiffened. The shame on his face was harsh, relentless. He looked at everyone, but no one could return his gaze. George, the only one with whom he had shared his story before today, looked ready to bolt, but his feet remained in place as he relived the agony of Jeff's tale.

"My neighbor Mark attacked my wife. She was lying on our garage floor when I came back, and he was ... doing things to her ..." Jeff paused as memories of that moment flooded back into his mind. He blotted them out and forced himself to continue.

"I took care of him, but there were others ... They had gotten inside and went after my kids."

A small moan escaped from Megan's throat as she shook her head even more furiously at Jeff, willing him to stop. She shoved her fist into her mouth to muffle the scream creeping up from her gut.

"I rushed through the house, but I was too late. So I dealt with the others that had invaded my home." He stepped closer to Megan. "But my children, my sweet angel Mary and my little Frankie ... they had already changed.

"I couldn't just leave them there, Megan. I had to ..." The tears rolled down his face as his voice broke. "They were my children! I loved them! I loved my wife. But I messed everything up. It was the only thing I could do for them. Give them peace. I couldn't let them stay like that. I couldn't!"

Megan rushed forward and wrapped her arms around Jeff. She tried to pull him tight, to cradle his head. She was willing to do almost anything to get him to stop speaking, to stop telling her these horrible things, but he grabbed her arms and gently pushed her back until he was looking into her eyes again.

"So I can't let Joey and Nathan suffer either."

Megan stiffened, realizing why he had told her all of this. She looked at Jeff, unable to think of anything to say. As she tried to move back into his arms, he resisted, holding her away. She wanted to comfort him, but his eyes were set. He was going to do this whether she wanted him to or not.

Her shoulders slumped, and after a moment, she nodded. It was the only blessing she could give. As she pulled away, Jeff let her go, watching as she walked to Jason and Sadie.

His eyes stayed on her for a moment longer, and then he looked at the other two men. George could barely make eye contact, still unable to grasp what Jeff had gone through with his family, even after hearing the story for the second time.

Ben had no such reservations. He wasn't certain, but he thought he had seen Nathan twitch. He knew what Jeff said was true. As the virus took control, the two boys would rise back up with no memory of who they were or of the people who had loved and cared for them. All they would know was hunger.

As he moved past Jeff, he whispered, "Make it quick."

Scooping up Sadie, Ben took a clean rag out of one of his many pockets and began wiping her off. He examined her for scratches and then gave her a small peck on the cheek. The five year old smiled up at him, happy to see Uncle Ben again as she snuggled into his arms.

The others followed as the bearded man waved them forward. George fell in line behind them as they moved down the street. Jeff remained, alone. Ben didn't bother telling him where they were going. He was expected to finish his task and catch up before the group was out of sight.

Jeff looked up into the sky and spotted a sliver of the moon. It was dusk and would be dark soon. He took a deep breath and looked at the two boys.

"Please forgive me."

He gripped the two by four George had left behind in both hands and moved toward Nathan, whose eyes were starting to open.

Chapter 21

It was almost nine o'clock, and darkness was finally closing in on the summer day when they made it to the building to which Ben had been leading them. Jeff caught up about half a block from where he left the boys. He hadn't taken long.

They only stayed in the building for a short time while Ben scouted ahead. No one spoke as they all slumped to the ground or leaned against shelves full of albums and compact discs in the used record store. The small, free-standing building was steeped in darkness due to the blacked-out front windows. The building had escaped much of the disaster that had befallen Manchester, with the old vinyl, cassettes, and CDs still nicely organized and all in place in the dusty aisles. Ben worked his way through the racks with relative ease despite the limited light.

Jeff gazed at the rest of the group as he leaned against a rack of old forty-fives and tried to come to grips with the fact that so many people had died that day. He overheard Jason whispering to George about the insurance office in which they'd hidden out, what happened to Teddy, and how Lydia had saved Megan from Cindy. Hearing Lydia's name stung Jeff as a vision of what he had done to her flashed through his mind.

Jason returned Jeff's weak smile when the boy looked his way and cradled his swollen elbow to his chest. The kid was in pain, but seemed to be in good spirits as he sat next to George and the two of them whispered back and forth.

Megan was more withdrawn as she held Sadie in her arms and ran her fingers through the girl's hair, though she seemed at peace.

Everyone looked up as Ben reappeared through the front door minutes later, closing it quietly as he turned to face the group.

"Okay, folks, let's head out. It's clear out front but won't be for long. Come on!"

Ben looked as pale and distraught as the rest of them. It did not reconcile with the quiet confidence the scout normally exuded. Jeff remembered the wink the man had given him when they first met and doubted he would be seeing another anytime soon.

Ben snapped his fingers a couple of times, breaking the deep trance that seemed to have settled over everyone. They were all wrung out and exhausted, but responded quickly enough as he gestured for them to follow. George reached over and helped Megan up, offering to carry the little girl. She smiled and shook her head as Sadie shifted in her arms so that her head lay on Megan's shoulder. Jeff wanted to speak to Megan, but couldn't think of anything that wouldn't push her even further away. He walked in silence behind the others as they left the record shop behind.

They spent the next hour and a half squirming through dark holes and creeping down back alleyways. Ben forced them to stop several times, his hand held up like a traffic cop. The sounds around them came and went as they wound their way through the town. The huddled group shifted closer to and then farther from the pockets of ghouls now wandering aimlessly after having lost track of anything that might lead them to food. None of Ben's followers knew the town very well, and in the moonlight, they were even less sure of themselves. They relied on him, despite the fact that on more than one occasion he took them in one direction then stopped sharply, listened for a moment, and executed a one-eighty to lead them down a different path. No one seemed interested in complaining as long as he continued to keep them safe.

They slid into several more anonymous buildings, the smell always dry and musty, with a hint of the same slaughterhouse funk that floated over the streets. Despite the near-pitch-black conditions inside each of the short-term shelters, Ben navigated his way through them efficiently.

It was obvious he'd previously been in at least some of the stopovers when he pulled out a backpack full of bottled water and snack crackers wedged behind a stack of chairs in a family restaurant. The crackers were chewy and stale and the water warm, but a feast of caviar and Dom Perignon would not have been better received by the group.

"How much longer are we going to be wandering around this shit hole?" Jason piped up between gulps of water.

Only small fingers of starlight showed through the gaps in the tarp that had been nailed over the plate glass windows. Everyone had adjusted to the gloom as Ben looked out the window closest to the door. The other adults waited for a response to the boy's question. Bullets of sweat poured down Ben's face as the light cast weird shadows across his visage.

"I mean, can't we just crash here for the night and get moving again in the morning? I don't see any reason for us to keep taking risks going outside and all."

Sadie had been awakened to eat, and she looked at Jason through droopy eyelids. His voice wasn't angry, although his eyes were weary with dim traces of fear. Everyone except the little girl watched and waited for Ben's response as he continued looking out the window. Sadie slid across the floor until she was next to Jason. He caught a glimpse of her out of the corner of his eye and looked down. She smiled and slid her tiny hand into his. He tensed as if he were going to resist her gentle offering, but then smiled back. The girl was filthy, covered with the debris of war, but her eyes drew him in, reassuring him. He gave her hand a squeeze as he looked at their guide.

The moments ticked by, and there was no answer. The other adults waited patiently for any kind of response from Ben, afraid to break his concentration or interrupt whatever strategies for their survival he was formulating in his head.

Ben let the tarp fall back over the window before turning to face the group. He had their undivided attention.

"We only have a little bit farther to go." Ben raised a hand to stop the protest he saw forming on several people's lips. "I know you're tired, but we're still in danger." He glanced at everyone in turn as he rubbed at his wrist nervously and wiped the sweat from his brow.

"Look, you just have to trust me for a little while longer. Do you think you can do that?"

When no one mounted a protest, Ben appeared to breathe a sigh of relief. Megan and Jason didn't look thrilled while George and Jeff seemed content to let Ben remain the group's designated leader for the time being.

After a couple more minutes, Ben motioned for them to stand up. Legs ached and knees popped, but there was no further protest as he led them back out onto the street.

Chapter 22

The brown, runty building to which they moved next housed several different businesses. They were in a chiropractor's office, having come through the rear entrance. Something about the road they were on seemed familiar to Jeff, though it was hard to pin down. It seemed as though the paltry group of refugees had been running through the entire town all day, and Jeff, like everyone else, had kept his eyes glued to Ben's broad shoulders instead of looking up at any street signs. They had left the asphalt fifteen minutes before and traveled alongside a set of railroad tracks. Ben had spun them around several times during their journey, but it was easy to surmise that they were gradually moving farther out from the center of town.

"Okay, everyone. Are you ready to make a break for it?" Ben said as they sat around the chiropractor's waiting room. The words caught everyone off guard.

"Break for it? What do you mean?"

Ben tried to smile. It looked funny on his lips, like it didn't belong there. He kept the grimace plastered on his face as he responded to Megan's question.

"You're getting out of here. Out of this godforsaken town. Tonight."

Ben dug into one of the deep pockets that lined his overalls and held two car keys out for display. He then gestured beyond the door to where two cars sat out on the street, ready and waiting.

"That old Corsica and Concorde ain't much to look at, but they both have full tanks."

Jeff rushed past Ben to the door and peeked out the window. He realized where they were. There was a line of cars outside the door, stretching about a quarter of a mile down the road. This was where the minivan had been trapped the day before, and the two cars were the ones that had been rolled into place to prevent Jeff's little contingent from escaping.

Goosebumps rose up on his skin as he saw several shapes moving amongst the shadows. Taking an involuntary step back, Jeff resisted the urge to move away from the window. There were more of them out there, yet all was quiet for the moment. He could only guess that most of ghouls that had attacked the camp had followed the RV as it drove into town, so there were only a few remaining in this area.

"But how are we supposed to drive out of here? There are too many wrecks and too many of those things out there." Despite Megan's doubt, it was apparent she was excited at the prospect of leaving Manchester and all the bad memories that dwelled there.

"I drew a map. Put it in the glove box of the Concorde. It doesn't have a huge amount of detail, but enough to give you a decent picture of things." The smile that had been plastered on Ben's lips faded. "It'll steer you clear of all the wrecks and the barriers folks put up around town. Steer you clear of most of the stiffs too ... at least enough that you should be able to drive on by them without any problems."

"Ben?" Jeff finally turned from the window. "It almost sounds as if you don't plan on coming with us." The words were hesitant, fearful.

Jeff watched as Ben shifted uncomfortably. There was a look of profound sadness on his face.

"You're not serious, are you? You have to come with us! At least if you expect us to somehow make it out of this godforsaken mess." Jeff grabbed Ben's arm as he fought to keep from screaming. But Ben was still shaking his head, resignation creeping across his bearded face.

"I ... I can't go with you."

"Why the hell not?" Megan shoved Jeff aside as she moved up, with George following. Ben raised a finger to his lips, urging her to lower her voice. Before she could recover from the stern warning, George chimed in.

"Ben, you know we need you. I'm not sure how far we can make it without you leading the way."

"You're not going with them either, George."

The words stopped them all cold. The argument forming on Jeff's lips, the angry invectives Megan was ready to spew out ... all came screeching to a halt.

"Wha-? What do you mean I'm not going with them?"

Jason jumped up. "What the hell are you talking about? George ain't leaving us!" His anger boiled to the surface in an instant, and Megan turned to the boy, her own irritation with Ben pushed to the side as she tried to put her hands on Jason's shoulders to calm the twelve year old down. He shrugged her off, the heat from his rage palpable.

Ben frowned as Jason tried to stand toe to toe with him. Both of the kid's fists were closed, though the effort was causing him a great deal of pain in his injured elbow.

Ben knelt before the gangly kid, his eyes filled with regret.

"George needs to get back to his family, Jason."

Jason hesitated. There hadn't been enough time to figure out why Ben made his proclamation about George, but now it was sinking in. After a moment, the fire returned to Jason's eyes.

"We're his family now, you stupid asshole!" Jason's fist rocketed off of Ben's chest. He hit him again, and Ben didn't try to stop the angry boy. He could see the tears ready to break free, but Jason fought to hold them back.

Strong, gentle hands gripped Jason's shoulders and turned him around. He resisted at first, his eyes still ablaze with anger at Ben. But as the boy turned to George, his expression shifted.

When he looked up at the man who had been his guardian for so long, there was fear in his eyes.

"You're not going to leave us, are you, George? Tell this idiot you want to stay with us!"

George could do nothing but stare at Jason, his mouth clamped shut.

"George? Tell him! Tell him there's no way you would leave us now! No way, no how!"

There were no more excuses ... except for the needs of the boy standing in front of him. Except for the love of all these people who had fought side by side with him through their journey into hell. And what else were they going to have to face? How many more desperate crazies? How many more of the infected? All without him, if he left. George wondered about Jeff, wondered how the man would do at protecting Jason and Megan once George was gone. The man was beaten down; he was no longer the arrogant bastard willing to risk them all just so he could take out a few more ghouls. But as Jeff had changed, so had Megan. There were underpinnings of strength in her that weren't readily apparent when they first met, yet had shone through in the past day. She could handle far more than he would have thought possible and had proven it time and again. Those two could handle things without him at their side. But could Jason?

George tried to formulate something to say, words that would make Jason understand, but he couldn't think of a single thing that would make the boy appreciate what he had to do. Because his mind was already made up. It was made up the instant Ben had said he wasn't going with the others.

"George?"

Jason watched as George's mouth opened and nothing came out. The twelve year old knew what the silence meant. He shook his head, the anger back. "No. You can't go! NO!"

George could think of nothing he could say to calm the boy, so instead, he grabbed Jason and pulled him close, wrapping his arms around him. The boy resisted, fighting against the strong arms, but George refused to let go, holding him closer, hushing him as Jason's words began to blend together. George heard words like 'hate' and 'die' and ignored them.

Jason kicked and tried to beat on him with his fist, but George kept him close until the kid calmed down.

"I love you, Jason ... and I'm sorry. If it could be any other way, I would do it, but I ... I have to get back to them. I have to be with them. Because I love them too. Because they don't have anyone watching out for them since I left. You still have Megan and Jeff. They'll do everything they can to keep you safe. Because I know they love you too."

The words were whispered, hushed, shared only by the two of them. Jason was too tired to keep fighting, and his head was throbbing. He could hear his pulse inside his ears along with George's heartbeat as he rested his head against his friend's chest.

"But I need you to stay, George. Please."

It was all he could get out before he began to cry. Jason held George tight with his good arm and drenched his shoulder with tears.

Neither of them spoke for a time as George held Jason close. The heartache he was feeling nearly overwhelmed the excitement stirring inside. He almost felt compelled to change his mind, to tell Ben no, that he would stay. But the images of his wife and two daughters were coming in stronger than ever. He had to get home. It was where he belonged.

When George thought the boy was okay, he gently pushed him back.

"I have to do this. It's my family. I can't abandon them. I have to go to them while I still have the chance."

There was pleading in his words, a desperate cry for approval. But Jason wouldn't give it, would not look up from the floor. As they separated, the sullen kid turned and slumped down next to Sadie, who had been watching everything stoically. She moved next to him and cuddled up. Jason immediately wrapped an arm around her and held her close.

George sighed and closed his eyes. When he opened them again, Megan was in front of him. Her anger at Ben's announcement was gone, replaced by disapproval and regret, but mostly resignation. She rubbed her arms as she shivered.

"Is this really what you want to do?" The words were barely audible. Not a whisper, like what he and Jason had shared. Her words were hoarse, worn so thin they were almost transparent.

When he nodded, she moved closer. George thought he was prepared for anything, but when she stepped in front of him and leaned her head into his chest, he was surprised. "I know how much you miss your family. Go to them." She looked up into his startled eyes and gave him a painful smile. "But don't you dare forget us."

George's lip quivered as he tried to return the smile. After failing, he slipped his arms around her and kissed her on top of her head. He had not realized how much tension there was in his body, how stressed he was over her possible reaction to his decision. Knowing that he had her blessing, even though she hated the idea of losing him, came with a profound sense of relief.

"I won't. I swear to God I'll never forget any of you."

"So what reason do you have for not coming with us?" Jeff's question sent all eyes toward Ben. Back in the spotlight, the big man looked uncomfortable with the attention. The sweat continued to pour down his forehead. Jeff inched forward. "You know we need you, Ben. I don't know if we can make it that far without you."

Ben stooped over the smaller man, and Jeff looked hesitant, but unafraid. When Ben moved his arm forward, Jeff flinched. Grabbing his hand, Ben pressed one of the keys into them.

"That's for the Concorde. It's already pointing east, which is the direction you want to head. The map is in the glove box. It's the bigger car, so it should be comfortable for the four of you. I put some things in the trunk that you guys will be able to use. Just pay attention to the map and you'll be fine." He leaned in close, his clammy fingers gripping Jeff's to make sure he had his full attention. "Don't panic, whatever you do. That's how a lot of folks died. They shit their pants at the first sign of trouble and were royally screwed."

Jeff's jaw was slack as Ben straightened his back and held his gaze steady.

"Can you do that, Jeff? Can you keep your cool?"

Jeff's mouth slammed shut, and he nodded. Whatever he planned on saying fled his mind as he looked up at Ben and realized how enormous the man truly was. But it was his eyes, his sad and terribly tired eyes, that told him arguing was pointless. Ben wasn't coming with them.

Ben handed George the other set of keys. "The Corsica is all the way down at the opposite end of the line of cars. I made sure it was gassed up and good to go, but I didn't bother putting any supplies in it. You'll just have to wing it. No map either, but I'm guessing you know where you're going."

George gave a quick nod, his gaze intense as he listened carefully. He looked at the key with the Chevy logo embossed on the fob. As he wrapped his fingers possessively around it, he looked nervous but ready.

Ben looked at George as if he were trying to convince himself that this was the right thing to do. After a moment, he returned the nod and addressed the rest of the group.

"Okay. Time's up. You folks have to get the hell out of here. We spend any more time jawin' and we're going to have company."

Ben shot a glance out the window and then turned back to the group. Everyone waited, breathless, for his next command. They were about as ready as they ever would be.

"I'll go out first. Just wait by the door and don't stick your head out until you're sure I've got their attention." He paused, eyeing the two other men. "You'll know when that happens. Wait about thirty seconds after that, then haul ass to the cars. The doors are unlocked."

Jeff and George nodded. Ben appeared satisfied that they understood his simple instructions. He turned back to the door. That was when he felt a little hand tugging on his fingers. It was Sadie, looking up at him with her bright eyes.

Without giving it any thought, he reached down and picked her up.

"Don't you want to come with us, Ben?"

The little voice and the needy look in Sadie's eyes tugged at Ben's heart. He felt almost dizzy as he held the little girl in his arms. He could handle the protests the adults might throw at him and even the bitter resentment that Jason felt, but he had to fight back the pain and guilt as he looked at the child he'd saved several weeks ago when she had been hiding out in a drainage ditch. He had never promised her that she would always be safe, but vowed to always do what he could to protect her. She was all that was left of the group he'd come to Manchester with, and now he was giving her to these people. For all they had been through together, he barely knew them. And yet, he knew in his heart that they would die doing everything they could to protect her, just as he would have done. He rubbed his cheek against the downy fluff of her hair as he closed his eyes.

"I can't come with you, baby. I wish I could; I really do." Sadie continued regarding him with those wide, haunting eyes, and he swallowed hard. "But Megan and Jeff are going to take good care of you. So is Jason. Aren't you?"

Megan came forward and smiled at the little girl as she caressed her chubby little arm. "We sure are, Sadie. Don't you worry about a thing."

Sadie's eyes moved back and forth between Ben and Megan, and then to Jason, who was still feeling betrayed by George's decision, but forced a faint smile to his lips for the little girl.

Sadie gripped Ben tight, kissing him on the cheek as she spoke into his ear. "Will I ever see you again?"

Ben squeezed his eyes shut and fought back the anguish that was a giant knot in his gut. He took a deep breath and held it for a few seconds before setting the little girl back down. He knelt before her and forced himself to look into her eyes as he spoke. "I tell ya what, honey. All you need to know is that you won't see me, but I'll always be around, watching out for you." He put on a brave smile for her. "You understand that, don't you?"

Sadie bobbed her head. The answer appeared to satisfy her and Ben began to stand back up. Before he could, she tugged on his sleeve again. "I'll miss you."

He smiled down at her again before turning back toward the door, where the smile crumbled. "Me too, baby. Me too."

Clearing his throat, Ben addressed the group. "Okay, everyone. It's time. No more screwing around. I'm going outside. Watch the window and wait about thirty seconds after I give you the signal. That'll give me enough time to stir these fuckers up."

Ben looked back one last time. They were fearful, but prepared for what they were about to face. He glanced at Sadie and saw that she fit perfectly in the crook of Megan's arm. Jason had moved next to them, his hand on Sadie's back. The kid still looked sullen and angry, but Ben knew he would get over it. Finally, he looked at Jeff and George. He nodded at them both as he opened the door.

There was no hesitation as Ben glided through the shadows, darting in between buildings and away from the cars. He was engulfed in darkness as the sounds of the night muffled his passing.

Chapter 23

Ben ached to his very bones, and his vision was blurry. His weary eyes felt like two raw eggs floating inside his skull. His breathing was ragged, and he could feel himself wearing down as he slid around a corner and stepped out onto the sidewalk. He licked his lips, knowing he didn't have much time.

He surveyed the street as he tugged on the zipper on the front of his coverall. When it was halfway down his chest, he reached inside to a pocket and grabbed the object he had tucked away earlier that day.

Smiling, he surveyed the street. It was not jam-packed, but there were enough ghouls to get things started. Ben glanced back toward the building where the last of the survivors waited for him to lead the monsters away from their doorstep. He had gone far enough to give them the room they needed. It was time to start making some noise.

He looked down at the .357 Magnum, and his grin widened. "Sorry, Megan. I know it's yours, but I needed to borrow it. Hope you don't mind." He inched out into the middle of the street and noticed that the sound of his voice had aroused some interest. Shadows shifted, and a face emerged into the moonlight. It moaned at him, curious.

"Well step out into the light and let me get a good look at you, son. Don't be shy."

Ben laughed as the greasy-looking man complied, excited to see him. As the shadowy figure moaned again, others responded, and there was more movement. A rainbow of gruesome colors was on display as more and more of the infected advanced on him. He swung around and looked them over, examining each in turn. The elements had not been kind to them. Even the ones that had not been torn to pieces were starting to look rather juicy.

Satisfied, Ben looked back toward the first rotter he'd seen. He waved him closer with the gun. "Come on, Lumpy, I ain't got all night."

The ghoul attempted to shuffle forward faster, but his right leg was twisted like a pretzel. "Well shit, pal. It must suck to be you. That gimpy leg must make it hard for you to catch dinner, huh?"

As the crippled stiff got closer, Ben could see that he was wearing the uniform of an auto mechanic or some other type of repairman. "Don" was stenciled on the jacket. Ben raised the gun and aimed carefully, unmoved by the sewn-in name. The man's name, like the rest of his life, had been destroyed once he was bitten and the virus took over.

"Sorry Lumps, but I can't wait any longer for you to get your screwed-up ass over here." Ben pulled the trigger. The gun exploded in his hands, sending a bullet through the creature's right eye. The man fell to the ground, ten feet from Ben.

He swung around, looking in all directions. "Now do I have everyone's attention?"

The stiffs were all on the move now, coming for him from every direction. Ben squinted in the dark back toward the survivor's hideout and saw that the small pack of ghouls that had been out front of the building were heading his direction. *Thirty seconds ...just wait another thirty seconds.*

He raised the gun again and shot the next shuffling stiff without ceremony. He lined up another shot and took aim.

"Sorry, no eulogy for you bastards," he mumbled as he continued firing.

Six shots fired. Ben had kept track. He had opened the cylinder earlier and doubled checked. The gun held seven rounds. There was one bullet left.

He heard an engine turning over and looked back toward the cars. Headlights flickered on. Jeff and Megan had made it to the

Concorde. He could only assume that George had made it to the Corsica as well.

Ben glanced down at his arm. Pulling back the sleeve of his coverall, he looked at the teeth marks on his wrist. Some dumb rotter had snapped at him when he'd grabbed Jeff in front of that donut shop. The bite had barely grazed his skin, but it felt as if acid were slowly eating away at his veins as the poison moved through his system. He laughed and shook his head. That was all it had taken to bring him down, after all this time.

Ben heard the roar of the Chrysler's engine, and the shadows dissolved briefly as the glare of the headlights whitewashed everything around him. Then the brilliance was gone, and the sound of the engine was already fading as the car turned off the road. Moaning replaced the mechanical sound as the beasts nearby drew closer.

Ben rubbed at the pus starting to come in thick teardrops from the corners of his eyes. He could hear slow footsteps all around him. As he raised the gun to his temple, he closed his eyes and prayed.

"Just give them a chance. I'm not asking for any miracles, just a chance."

When he felt the first of the scratching fingers grab for him, Ben pulled the trigger.

Chapter 24

The first shot made them jump.

"Holy shit! Where the hell did that come from?"

Jeff looked out the window, but couldn't see anything that would shed any light on what had happened. For a fleeting moment he considered the possibility that someone besides Ben was out there.

"It sounds like my revolver," Megan said as she walked up behind him.

As Jeff scanned the darkness he saw several shadows pass and was shocked at how many infected were still in the immediate area.

He nearly jumped out of his skin when a hairless and naked ghoul walked right past the door, not two feet from where he stood. When it kept moving, not even giving a sideways glance to the door, Jeff breathed easier.

He turned back toward the others. "Okay. Once those things are clear of the cars, we're moving out."

The two other adults and Jason looked at him and nodded. His eyes lingered on Megan, who had Sadie in her arms. She looked calm and ready to go. As she glanced at Jeff, he looked away, the sting of what he had told her about his family rumbling through his mind.

Instead, he looked at George. The man was almost vibrating in anticipation. He was as nervous as the rest of them, but his eyes were clear and alert.

"George, can you come to our car first?" George looked puzzled at the request. "Help me get everyone inside, and we can make sure the path to your car is clear. If it isn't, we'll drive you to it."

George thought for a moment before responding, and then nodded. "That makes sense. Sure."

Jeff turned around. When Megan's Magnum barked a second and third time, he was not caught off guard. He counted to ten under his breath. It looked clear outside. There were a few sluggish bodies dragging themselves toward the sounds of gunfire on the opposite side of the street, but nothing they couldn't handle. When Jeff got to ten, he gripped the door handle.

"Everyone ready?" He waited, his heart thumping in his chest. When he heard the whispered acknowledgements, he opened the door and moved out on the street.

The night was thick with humidity. The faint whiff of decay that permeated the air was hardly noticeable to the survivors anymore. They moved silently and swiftly toward the car. Jeff did not bother looking back, trusting that George would be on the lookout for any danger signals from behind. As the revolver barked again, Jeff nearly jumped out of his shoes. The sound, unimpeded by the closed door, came at them like thunder.

They made it to the Concorde with no problems, although Jeff thought he spotted several sets of eyes tracking them. He fumbled for the keys as Megan opened the back door and slid Sadie inside. Instead of following the child, she turned and surprised George with a hug. It was a quick squeeze that he barely had a chance to return. "You'll never know how much we'll miss you, George."

She couldn't look at him as she turned and opened the front passenger door and slid inside. George watched as she did, blinking in the starlight.

Jason stood next to him, awkward and uncomfortable. He still looked sullen, his mouth quivering as he glared at George.

"Stay strong, Jason. Jeff's going to need you to step up and watch over Sadie and Megan."

Suddenly, the anger and bitterness were swept away, and all that was left was a frightened little boy.

"Don't go, George," he pleaded. "You can still come with us! You can still change your mind. Just get in the car. We'll find your family together! There's no reason for you to leave us!"

"It's too dangerous. I can't ask you to come with me. I have to do this on my own."

Jason opened his mouth again, but no words came out. He was still shaking his head in disbelief when George pulled him into his arms and gave him a hug.

"I just can't believe you're really leaving," Jason whispered after a few moments, his voice stunned. "I'm never going to see you again, am I?"

It was as hard for George to accept as it was for Jason to say. But there it was. There were words he wanted to say, promises he wanted to make, but they would be lies, stupid little wishes. Once he left, there would be no turning back and no way to find the others again. When he and Jason finally broke off their hug, George shook his head.

There were no more words. Jason turned and slipped into the car beside Sadie, shutting the door behind him.

"It looks clear to your car."

Jeff had been acting as lookout as George said his farewells. There were bodies moving out there, but none between the two cars, as far as he could tell. Another gunshot exploded in the night as George squinted, searching for the Corsica. He spotted it and nodded at Jeff. He patted his pants pocket, making sure he still had the key.

"I hope you find your family, George. I really do."

There was a trace of wistfulness in the words. Jeff wanted to believe, for George's sake, that his family, beyond all fathoming, was still alive.

George looked at Jeff and saw the pain that still resonated behind his eyes. It had been a rough day for all of them, but it had taken more of a toll on Jeff than on any of them.

"Give her a chance."

Jeff's eyes narrowed in confusion at George's plea.

"Give Megan a chance to understand. She will, you know. If you give her time."

Jeff's face reddened with embarrassment and anger. He looked away and wondered if his thoughts were that obvious.

"Jeff, we've all done things ..." George hesitated as he tried to piece together something that would make his friend understand. "We've all done horrible things that we feel like we can't live with, that no one could ever forgive us for." He stepped closer and forced Jeff to look him in the eyes. "But you have to forgive yourself for what you've done. Because Megan already has."

Jeff nodded, though George wasn't sure if the other man was agreeing or just placating him. It was clear Jeff had been damaged by the events of the past few days—even the past few hours—but George could hope the damage wasn't irreparable. He knew that if anyone could help him heal, it was Megan.

He held out his hand. Jeff looked at it and only hesitated for a split second. The anger left his face while the embarrassment remained. This was goodbye. Jeff forced a smile onto his face. "You're a good friend, George. I'm going to miss you."

George nodded. "Me too." He squeezed Jeff's hand tighter for a moment. "Take care of them. They need you now more than ever."

Jeff nodded. "I will. No matter what happens, you can count on that."

It was not an easy thing to do, but George let go of the other man's hand and ran to the Corsica.

Jeff watched while circling to the driver's-side door and kept on watching until George climbed into the other vehicle. By the time the sixth shot rang out, he was behind the wheel of the Concorde and starting it up.

Megan had the map out of the glove box and was ready to navigate. Jeff looked in the back seat and saw that both kids were buckled up, ready to go. Jason had a distant look in his eyes, as if his mind was already far away. He had his arm around Sadie, who was leaning on him with her feet curled up beneath her little body. She was already slipping off to sleep again, and Jeff was amazed at how easy it was for the little girl to do that.

He glanced over at Megan as he flipped on the lights. "You ready?"

"As I'll ever be." A small smile crossed her face as she reached over and took hold of his hand, squeezing it. "Let's get out of here."

Jeff smiled back at Megan and thought about what George had said, about giving her the time to understand.

Several ghouls stopped when they saw the lights and heard the engine come to life. Jeff easily avoided them as he drove down the street, listening to Megan's voice as she read the map and told him where he needed to turn. The directions would take them out of town and a few miles into the country. The path Ben had laid out was a series of residential streets, away from the crowds, wrecks, and barricades that would hamper their movement.

Another shot rang out, and Jeff's thoughts turned back to Ben. He wanted to remember everything he could about him. Perhaps he would write it all down someday: the journey he'd taken and the people he'd met. Otherwise, memories of the hulking man and even of George would fade. They would become myths for those who lived, if they were remembered at all. Jeff stared out onto the road as he thought about it. *So many people I don't want to forget. So many people I should never forget.* Even the ones he despised needed to be remembered. If they were lucky enough to meet anyone else on their journey, their stories needed to be told.

As they turned off the main road and diverged into a residential neighborhood, Jeff felt some of the burden of what had happened in Manchester over the past day slip off his shoulders. They were still alive. It defied all logic, but they were.

Megan looked over at him, her hand sliding across the console to touch his arm. As he glanced over at her, there was a solemn look on her face.

"Remind me to tell you about what happened to my husband sometime."

Jeff stared at her for another moment, the surprise evident on his face. Then he nodded as his eyes moved back to the road. Megan's fingers ran down his arm until they reached his hand. She gave him a quick squeeze before letting go.

*

As they moved past the quiet residential neighborhoods and out into the country, Jeff scanned the horizon. The road ahead was dangerous. There was no way of knowing where it would lead them. Perhaps there was some safe haven where they could forget the world for a time. Even if just for a brief while. But Jeff didn't want to dwell on the idea. Being alive for the time being was good enough.

"Do you think we'll make it, Jeff?"

It was a question that could drive them insane if they let it.

"I don't know," Jeff said quietly. "But I remember something someone told me once. At the time it sounded a bit hokey, like it was out of some sort of self-help manual, but as I think about it now, it seems to ring true. They said live this day as if it will be your last. You will only find tomorrow on the calendar of fools."

Jeff glanced at Megan and could see that she was trying to absorb what he had said. She nodded after a moment.

"Honestly, Megan, I don't know." He hesitated. "But we have each other. I think that's all we can ask for."

*

As they drove on into the night, Jeff's words echoed in Megan's head. They were in uncharted waters, but they had each other. All they could do was take it one day, one hour, one moment at a time. Somehow, she could accept that.

The road up ahead was dark and dangerous, but for some reason, it did not frighten Megan anymore.

Epilogue, Part 1

The roads were obstacle courses forcing him to keep the car below thirty miles per hour and even slower when he came upon one of the dozens of smash-ups along the rural routes. The four-cylinder engine huffed and groaned at him as he switched his right foot from the gas pedal to the brake again. At least there weren't a lot of ghouls in the area.

George figured most were behind him, back in the town he had left behind for good. The car, a rusted Chevy Corsica that was nearly twenty years old, smelled like mothballs and ancient sweat. It wheezed and protested as he urged it along, rattling and threatening to fall apart, but it kept moving. The headlights and the engine worked, and that was good enough for him.

As the buildings disappeared in the rearview mirror along with the few stiffs trying to take swipes at him, George relaxed. There were more small towns up ahead, but he knew the roads well enough to avoid most of the trouble spots. Most of them. He would still have to figure out how to navigate past Willowsburg and the interstate.

Willowsburg was probably four or five times the size of the town he'd just left. He racked his brain for an alternate route around it, but unless he wanted to go off road, hit even more population, or go on foot, he had to go through Willowsburg. The road leading home went right through the town.

It was the interstate that really worried him. Everything George knew, everything he had heard, was that the highways were a complete mess. Gridlock from one exit to the next even with the National Guard cordoning off large chunks. Massacres everywhere, thousands dead as they attempted to flee in every direction while their cars remained stuck. Interstates were to be avoided at all costs.

His home was on the other side of the interstate that cut across the entire state.

The old car ate away at the miles, the headlights slicing through the darkness on the two-lane road as it rolled along. There were a few stalled vehicles—abandoned or incapacitated. George avoided looking too closely at them, though it was hard to miss the fact that some had been attacked. Even out here in the country where the population was sparse, there had been plenty of devastation. Farmhouses burnt to the ground, fire pits where bodies had been rudely tossed, and even executions.

George could not help but slow down as he passed a huge, gnarled old tree. The limbs were thick and sturdy, strong enough to hold the weight of several people. The tree was alive and vital, but on its branches were several hanging ropes. A few dangled freely, the ends frayed as if they had been hacked or chewed at. But it was the others, the ones that hung taunt that captured George's attention.

The three bodies, hung at various heights, pitched and weaved at the sight of the car. There was no moaning, just jittery movement. George wanted to look away, but couldn't tear his eyes from them. As he watched them gyrate and dance, their arms tied behind their backs, necks broken and distended, he wondered how long they had been up there.

No one deserves that. No one. George stopped the car, his grip on the steering wheel painful as he watched a young girl attempt to open her mouth as her eyes bugged out. She could not accomplish the simple task with a rope snug beneath her chin. It had worn through her soft skin and throat muscles and kept her jaw from moving. Much of the skin had been picked clean from her face or had dissolved in the summer heat, George could not tell which. She wore what must at one time have been a pretty print dress, and a pair of patent leather shoes lay on the ground below her.

It must have been a slow journey to hell for the people hanging on the tree. George tried to comprehend who would have done such a thing, tried to absorb what possible reason there was to prolong these people's agony. As he counted the ropes, he saw that there was a total of seven; seven people had been hung out on this country road. For what reason? As a symbol? As an attempt to stir up fear? Were they already dead or merely freshly bitten when they were lynched? George rubbed his eyes as he sat back in his seat and sighed. He looked past the tree and could see a house off in the distance. He wondered if the people who had lived there had taken the answers to the grave ... or if they were the ones dangling from the tree.

There's no time. Not enough time to make this right, not enough time to make any of it right. George forced his eyes back onto the road as he pressed down on the gas pedal and sped off into the night, leaving the three hanging bodies twitching in the humid summer air.

A few miles later, George was able to turn off the rural route and hit a much wider state road. Still only two lanes, but plenty of space. Plenty of room to avoid the rusting junk piles that were more spread out here. As he turned off the rutted country path and felt the smooth asphalt beneath the tires, he knew he was about fifteen miles from Willowsburg ... and fifteen more after that from home.

Home.

The thought electrified him. *All this time and I've been so close.* He could have run so long ago. But time seemed to slow down and then speed up day after day, moment after moment. He'd lost perspective on how long he had been away. It had been eternity and yet only a single moment. The urgency ebbed and flowed as desperation and fear struggled with one other.

Have they waited for me? Are they still waiting for me?

As George drove, he focused his eyes on the broken yellow lines he passed. The road was clear ahead, and at the end of it was home.

***

IF YOU DIED TODAY, WHERE WOULD YOU SPEND ETERNITY?

The headlights flashed over the words on the billboard outside the tiny little township that George thought was named Slugo or something like that. Sligo? Slaygo? Slaygo—now wouldn't that be perfect? Whatever signs had served to tell travelers the name of the town were all gone—demolished or flattened to the ground amongst rusting iron sentinels on the side of the road. Not just cars and pickups anymore; there were a couple of tractors to add variety to the mix. George wondered if someone had the bright idea of trying to flee on a tractor. One was toppled, lying on its side like a dead elephant, its shattered bones and flattened tires looking sad and pathetic while the other, farther up the road, was still upright and parked at an angle next to the road. It was a lonely sentinel guarding a whole lot of nothing.

HELL IS REAL!

George nodded at the next billboard, printed in the same white block letters as the previous one.

"It sure is."

He remembered seeing them all over the place, up and down the highways, as ubiquitous as the God Speaks billboards a few years ago, with their catchy little phrases like "Don't make me come down there." He tried not to laugh as he thought about it. God had come down. God came down and dealt out retribution with no discrimination between who was good and who was evil. Almost everyone had been consumed in the conflagration. Almost.

George's eyes drooped, and as the car gradually moved toward the edge of the road, he jumped in his seat, straightening the wheel. It had been happening more and more over the past hour. He had no idea what time it was, but the wreck, if that was the correct term for the massive pileup a few miles back, had forced him to take a three-hour detour. It had reminded him that there were still plenty of slugs out there, buried in the backwoods and on every dirt road. For a time, the gravel kicking up and hitting every part of the undercarriage kept him awake. That and the winding path he had been forced to take and on which he had promptly gotten lost. Every time he thought he was about to jump back on the main road, it ended up leading him on another wild goose chase, farther away from his goal. Finally, after fearing that he was never going to get back on track, he recognized a minor landmark. It was a convenience store he remembered from previous trips through the area. It stood alone on a remote crossroad with a dead yellow light up above as its only company. That and the cornfields that ran in all directions. He knew where he was: a mere two miles farther down the road than he had been when he was forced to take his extended detour.

The air conditioner didn't work. Not that George was surprised, but he hoped a continuous blast of cold air would help keep him awake. Avoiding a few infected that got close to the car when he was on the dirt roads kept him alert for a time. Now, back on the smooth asphalt, there was little to keep his attention.

He rolled down the windows, but he could not speed up enough to get much of a breeze going. The road would be clear and then, out of nowhere, another obstacle would materialize: a car, a dead animal, or just a rotten hunk of meat covered in flies. There had been no attempts at an ambush. No sightings of another living soul, in fact. If there was anyone still left in this area, they were staying out of sight and off the road.

At least if he were forced to deal with someone else, it might help keep him awake.

*

"Wake up, you idiot!"

George slapped himself in the face. Two quick raps that stung for a moment, though the pain dulled far too quickly. He was weaving all over the road, exhausted. He was not sure where he was, or what he was doing. As he shook his head and widened his eyes, he roared in frustration. Hitting the brakes, he slammed his head against the steering wheel.

"You are on your way back home. Your name is George Montgomery. Your wife and kids are waiting for you, you stupid son of a bitch! Get your shit together before you kill yourself!"

The anger produced a spurt of adrenaline, enough to make George hyperaware of his surroundings for a few moments. He was on the road leading to Willowsburg, only a few miles away from what might be the most dangerous part of his trip.

He scanned the road. There had been a few businesses along the way, but the road was mostly flanked with houses, set back in the distance. There were a lot of trees that offered a limited view of most of the properties on both sides. Entire groves in some instances.

George slid the car off to the side of the road. *Maybe a short rest will do the trick. Just a few minutes. Something to jumpstart me.* He pulled up under a rather impressive poplar that towered over the car. A nice quiet spot. For just a few minutes.

Resting his hand on the key, he turned it and let the car die. He waited, listening, wondering when they would start moving in his direction. They were out there. They were a part of the fabric of everything these days, so they had to be out there. He locked the doors and rolled up the windows, making sure they were not open even a crack. He felt more awake in that moment than he had for several hours. It made no sense, but he accepted it like he accepted almost everything else. There was nothing he could control any longer, not even his own eyelids.

George put his hands on the steering wheel. He had seen no movement. He was sure the car had been heard, though perhaps the dead had no way of pinpointing the source of the noise. With the windows closed, they might not be able to smell him either. The living, on the other hand ... well, if someone was out there, hiding, waiting to pounce on him, there was little he could do about it. He could not drive any farther. Getting closer to the town without his nerves as sharp as they needed to be would spell certain doom, especially in the dark.

What time was it? It had to be four in the morning, perhaps later. When would the first light of dawn peek over the horizon? He was facing the right direction, almost due east. If he closed his eyes, the sun would serve as a natural alarm clock ...

as long as something else didn't wake him before that. If it did, he would be ready. A quick move of his hand, and the car would be moving again. George found it hard to believe that enough stiffs could sneak up on him to make a quick getaway too difficult.

Just a few minutes. As the reassuring thought made one last pass through his brain, his eyes fluttered and his head slid back onto the headrest.

*

There were bells. It was a strange noise, because George had been dreaming of the church in which he had been stuck for so long. This was not the sound of church bells, though. Nothing as grand as that. It was simpler, someone clanging some cheap copper rig, its ringer sloppily banging against the side.

When he opened his eyes, he almost screamed. A long, sad face was staring at him from outside the window. He was awake in an instant, though he had no idea what was going on. He grabbed for the key, knowing somehow that was what he was supposed to do. As he fumbled for it, the large Holstein staring in at him rubbed the window with its big, wet nose.

George peered out at the cow and let his heart settle in his chest. The big bell around its neck clanked out its off-key little tune as the beast licked the window and then moved away. *Good gravy, George, you almost got eaten by a cow.* The thought of an undead cow brought a smile to his lips as he stretched in his seat. His back was stiff, but he felt good, awake and coherent for the first time in days. The latest layer of sweat that drenched his clothes didn't bother him, even though, with the windows closed, he felt as if someone were warming him up like leftovers.

Sunlight streamed into the car. As George looked out over the quiet landscape, he was surprised to see that the area in which he'd stopped was not marred by the damage and wreckage that were so commonplace everywhere else he'd been. He rolled down his window and stuck his head out. He had slept well past dawn. The sun was not at its zenith, but it was creeping toward it, away from the east.

He considered the cow. It looked unscathed and fairly content as it munched on some grass. Not sick or wounded. In fact, it looked fat and healthy. Given the infecteds' indiscriminant desire to attack any living thing, the cow was an anomaly.

Willowsburg was just a few miles down the road. Its infected population would have burst free from the city limits long ago and poured through the countryside, tearing through every last bit of livestock. George wiped the sleep out of his eyes. He had slept several hours longer than he had planned and still had a ways to go before he was home. This mystery would just have to go unsolved. He had to keep moving.

As he started the car back up, the cow sauntered farther away, its bell clanking its lonely call. The cow might be still alive, but it was alone. *Probably just been lucky so far. The rest of the herd is probably already dead.* "Sorry, Bessie, I wish I could help you out." As he pulled back out onto the road, the cow raised its head from the grass it was munching and lowed at him as if to respond to his sentiment.

George took a deep breath and gripped the steering wheel. He would have to find a way through Willowsburg. The car was not in the best shape, but it didn't seem likely to give out on him just yet. There was still more than half a tank of gas left in it, even after his little side trip the night before.

As he drove along, he saw a wide-open expanse off to his right. From the corner of his eye, it looked like any other open field, covered with black loamy dirt. But as the car passed by, thousands of birds took off, startled by the vehicle. The black mass was far larger than any flock he'd ever seen. They had covered every square inch of the flat space that spread away from the road at least a quarter of a mile. He watched in awe as the flock cast a massive shadow over the car on its way north, away from the disruption that had upset it. He could hear the beating of wings as the birds cawed, angry with him. The field they left behind was drab, brown, and barren of life.

He was still thinking about the great flock of birds as he moved closer to Willowsburg. Thinking about the cow and what other animals might still be nearby, somehow escaping the threat of the undead. As he neared the town, he understood why things seemed so peaceful.

Willowsburg had burned to the ground.

He didn't know whether he should be relieved or saddened by the complete destruction of the town of over twelve thousand. It appeared as if no structure had gone untouched. Even the houses that lined the road a couple miles from town were burnt down to their foundations. As he moved in closer, driving through the downtown area, he was overwhelmed by the charred remains. The fire, or fires, had been thorough, wiping the slate clean. The weather had been dry as a bone over the past couple of months. Once the fires had started, there was nothing to stop them until they'd burned themselves out.

As George left the last of the cooked structures behind, he felt sad. No one would ever know what had happened here. There was no one left to tell the story. The town was dead, cremated. In time, it would be as if it never existed.

Sorrow overwhelmed the slight relief he felt that one of the places he had feared the most in his journey had become nothing more than an unmarked grave. This was someplace close to home, the place where he had lived for years. He knew no one who'd lived in Willowsburg, but he had passed through the town many times over the years. There was a hollow, empty feeling in the pit of his stomach as he thought about how many places this might have occurred ... and that it might have happened in his own town. The thought of his wife and baby girls trapped as fire raged all around them was unbearable. George pushed down harder on the gas pedal, spurring the car onward.

He had one more major barrier, one more place to pass. The highway crossed the road just a few miles away. Past that, there were more farms and trees but not much else. There was a little dimple in the road that no one would argue was a town, but that was it. After the interstate, he was home free.

*

The landscape changed as the burnt remains of Willowsburg became a dark smudge in the rearview mirror. The scorched earth was replaced with dry grass and old trees that had survived both the fire and the undead. George sucked in air between his teeth as he saw a highway overpass off in the distance. Even from almost a mile away, he could see the shapes of cars crowding onto it.

As he drew closer, there was a spill of cars on the exit ramps: people who had been trying to get off the highway while others were trying to get on. Many had died in their cars. He could see skeletal remains and fierce clouds of flies swarming the last few pieces of meat inside the vehicles. There were some skeletons, but many who died must have gotten back up and wandered off, attacking others who were stuck in the traffic stretching for miles in both directions.

George knew the exit had a couple of gas stations and a row of fast food joints that lined both sides of the road. You could pick your poison. The big hitters were all there: McDonald's, Wendy's, Taco Bell, KFC, Burger King, and a Bob Evans thrown in for good measure. George relaxed when he saw that the middle of the road was clear, granting him room to pass. There were cars everywhere: the side of the road, in the parking lots— a few were even flipped over on the median.

The area was quiet and had a vacated feel to it. Any of the living who had survived the initial assault that had conquered this little niche off the highway had fled long ago. With their food source gone, the flesh eaters must also have departed.

As George looked out over the fast food havens and daydreamed about the days long past when his girls would beg him to take them to McDonald's for a Happy Meal, a woman walked out the front door of the Taco Bell. George did a double take, unsure if he had really seen her. The doors to the Mexican joint were far away, and he slowed the car down as he gawked in her direction. Squinting in the sunlight and blinking, he tried to focus on her.

She looked normal in the sunlight. George's eyelids narrowed further. The movement was regular, her legs steady underneath her as she walked out into the parking lot. There was no blood and no discoloration to her skin. Her hair was long and dark, falling straight around her head. Her face looked unharmed: two eyes, a nose … no bones peeking through. It looked like she was scanning the cars that surrounded her. It appeared as if she hadn't noticed the old Chevy moving down the road toward her just yet.

George looked over at the doors of the Taco Bell. Seeing inside was impossible with the glare bouncing off the large sheets of glass that wrapped the front of the building. None of the windows was shattered. There was no plywood up either, no makeshift barricades he could see. If that was where the woman had been hiding, she must not have been there very long. Looking back at her, he saw that she wasn't carrying any weapons and was wearing shorts and a filthy t-shirt. Nothing that would protect her from any sort of attack.

Pressing the brake, George brought the car to a stop. He gripped the steering wheel as his foot twitched, ready to return to the gas pedal if necessary. Memories of the ambush from a couple of days earlier had him nervous. But even as he looked from restaurant to restaurant, waiting for some kind of trap to be sprung or someone to come rushing out to attack him, he let the car continue to idle.

Nothing moved. Even after he swore he saw a shadow twitch near the Wendy's, there was nothing. His eyes went back to the woman. She was looking in his direction now, but he couldn't see any reaction. Her age was hard to guess. Lank, greasy brown hair clung to her face and allowed two larger-than-normal ears to stick out.

Letting out a slow hiss of breath, George moved his foot off the gas pedal and let the car inch forward. As he did, he rolled down the window and stuck his head out to speak to the woman.

There was no smile on her face, no excitement at seeing him, but no fear either. He watched as she plucked at her shirt with her right hand repeatedly. The cotton had almost worn through where she touched it. George moved close enough to see her eyes and knew for certain. They were the same dull, watered-down brown as her hair. Uninspiring, but more importantly, uninfected. He put his foot back on the brake and stopped the car a few feet from her. He put on a smile that he hoped didn't look threatening.

"Hello! I'm sure glad to see you!"

Any concerns he had about being deceived, or of getting

trapped, evaporated.   Instead, there was an almost overwhelming urge to connect with someone who was still alive. The pain at leaving Jason and the others felt like a rusty knife digging into his gut. Seeing this girl up close made George realize how desperate he still was for human contact.

She didn't stop moving or react to the words. For a moment, George stiffened, and his foot screamed to be allowed off the brake. *Roll up the window! Hit the gas! Get out of here now!* But the feeling passed when, instead of moans, words escaped her lips.

"Mel? Where's Mel?" The girl's voice startled him as she leaned forward and looked in through George's open window. The words were a squeak, barely audible, yet they blindsided him nonetheless. She continued to lean forward, her hands resting on the door as she ignored George. Without even thinking about it, he moved farther into the car, his body pulling away as her head popped through the window frame.

"Ma'am? Are you-"

"Mel! Quit hiding and get out here before I tan your hide!"

The increased volume rattled George even more than the aggressiveness with which the woman forced her head into the car. She looked like a ghost—thin, pale, and tall, with an almost boyish figure. She was young, with acne scars running across her cheeks like constellations. Her teeth were a dingy yellow, matching her jaundiced complexion. She smelled of dirt and grease.

"Lady, what the hell are you doing? Mel's not in here!"

The words spilled out, blurted without thinking as George shrank back in his seat from the young woman, who likely weighed no more than a hundred pounds, bulling her way in through his window.

She continued screaming, the words angry and irrational as she yelled for Mel and pushed past George. She reached and grabbed, her dirty and ragged fingernails scratching him as she did.

"Stop it. Get the hell away from me, you crazy bitch!"

The hard shove that accommodated the words knocked the deranged woman back out of the car and dumped her to the asphalt. To George, she felt like a bundle of dried sticks. He watched as she slid across the road and sat, stunned.

He didn't know what to do. His heart was racing and he felt guilty. Almost involuntarily, he looked around, embarrassed at his brutal response to her inane inquiries. It was foolish, but he was worried someone might have seen what he'd done. He put the car in park, opened the door, and stepped out. Holding out his hand, he moved toward the woman.

"I'm sorry ma'am. Are you okay? Did I hurt you?"

As he moved forward, the disheveled woman scooted backwards, trying to regain her feet and stay clear of George at the same time. She was finally looking directly at him, and her eyes were much clearer now, focused. He wondered if she had snapped out of whatever daydream she'd been having. He stopped moving and kept his hands where she could see them.

"Are you all right?"

She lifted herself up off the ground. There were a few new scratches on her legs, but nothing major. George felt more guilt and wanted to help her up, but was afraid to get closer. Especially as he saw the look on her face.

The sudden change of expression was unnerving. The transition from hazy bewilderment and befuddled determination to animalistic rage took less than a second. Now it was George's turn to backpedal.

"What did you do to Mel, you motherfucker?"

The words were laced with acid, and spittle flew from her dry lips. Her fingers curled into claws, and her dingy teeth were looking more menacing by the second. There was hatred in her eyes the likes of which he had never seen before. A lunatic abhorrence reserved for murderers and rapists. Even Cindy had looked tame by comparison. The woman took a step forward.

"Lady, I don't know who Mel is, and I didn't do a thing to him!"

George slid back into the car. Any thought of helping this deranged creature was gone—chewed up and spit out with her instant mania. George almost fell back into his seat as she closed on him.

Thankfully, he hadn't turned off the car. Slamming the door

shut, he rolled up the window. The woman came up to the window and glared at him with malignant eyes. George guessed that she wasn't infected with the virus, but with a madness that was probably just as dangerous.

Without preamble, she banged on the window and screamed. The words were laced with curses and profanity as she spit and scratched, screaming for Mel. George was shaking as he put the car back into drive. He flinched as the window vibrated under her blows.

Even as he pulled back onto the road, the woman stayed next to the car, demanding to know where Mel was. George's head swam as she cried out, shouting the name over and over again. He kept his eyes forward and tried to ignore her, but it was impossible.

As the car continued to roll forward, he spotted movement off to his right. He took his eyes off the road long enough to make out several shambling forms inside the KFC. As he surveyed the area, he could see more movement from one of the gas stations and another fast food joint.

George put on the brakes again. The woman, who had been picking up speed in an effort to keep up with the car, came to an abrupt halt and was silent for a moment as she was caught off guard. The Corsica's idle wasn't whisper quiet, but it was easy to hear the sounds of moaning at this distance.

"Give me back my baby, you bastard! I'll rip your eyes out if you don't give me my baby!"

George no longer feared the crazy woman; he feared *for* her. Driving away and leaving her alone in her madness was no longer an option. He braced himself as he reached for the door handle.

His eyes never left her as he stepped free of the car once again. There was movement all over now, not just from the KFC or gas station. The woman's voice and the sound of the car's engine had carried, echoing up and down the highway. It was obvious that undead that probably had been hibernating for weeks were now awake, just like they had been awoken back in Manchester.

George prepared for whatever attack this hopeless woman might launch at him. He pushed on the car door as she leaned against it, hoping to knock her back to the ground. The girl was more nimble than he expected and moved back quickly enough to avoid the door. As George stepped out onto the street, the madwoman continued to backpedal. Her eyes were livid, still filled with the mysterious anger that fueled her, but she also looked skittish, unsure of herself.

George moved forward, not wasting any time with useless diplomacy. "You have to come with me, miss. Those things are coming."

George pointed back at where he had seen the shadowy figures as they dragged their carcasses out from their hiding places. The woman flinched when he moved, perhaps fearing he was planning to attack her. She kept moving backwards, shaking her head as she started to cry.

"You killed Mel. Why? Why did you kill him? You killed my baby!"

George shook his head, doing his best to roll with her vacillating emotions. Sweat trickled down his back. He crept forward, his nerves shot as his mind raced with different ideas of how to get this woman to climb into the Corsica with him.

"Keep back! Stay away from me!"

She looked poised to run. Her legs were bent, and if he continued coming for her, she would take off, away from him and into the arms of dead. She seemed completely oblivious to the danger she was facing.

George froze and lowered his hands. He took one last look around the area and noticed that the only building in sight without bodies filing out the doors and shattered windows was the Taco Bell where the woman had been hiding. They were running out of time.

"I didn't kill Mel. I swear I did not kill your baby. But ..." He looked her in the eye, hoping that she saw the sincerity in his gaze. "But if you come with me, maybe we can find him. Maybe he's not dead."

George had no idea where the spontaneous lie had come from, but after he spoke the words, he held his breath, waiting and hoping for some kind of positive reaction. For a moment, there was a spark in her eyes, something like lucidity that hadn't been there before. It was a brief shining instant, perhaps the only one this poor soul had experienced in a very long time, in which she was sane again, and understood what had happened to her and what she had become.

The moment passed, and the haze that had gripped the woman fell upon her like the closing of a window shade. She turned and ran. George moved forward a few steps and screamed after her, pleading for her to return, but whatever moment of understanding she had gained was gone, and she was lost for good.

She ran back to the Taco Bell, pulling the door open and sliding into the dark shadows inside the dead restaurant. Already, some of the ghouls that had been shambling toward the Corsica were changing course to follow her.

George paused, his throat hoarse as he cried out to the woman one last time. The stiffs that hadn't adjusted their trajectory were still headed in his direction. The path to the girl was already close to being blocked off. At least a dozen infected were already crossing the parking lot, while more than twice as many were headed in his direction.

George could hear moans from all sides, but no screams. Not yet. His shoulders sagged as he turned back to the car and slid behind the wheel. He wouldn't wait for the screams. Not this time.

Part 2

Six weeks earlier ... June 30th

"What's happening? What the hell is wrong with everyone?"

"I don't know, honey. It's crazy everywhere. Everyone here is freaking out and wants to go home, just like me."

There was a pause. George tried counting his heartbeats, which he could hear as his hand quivered around the cell phone. He could feel the pulse beats in his hand, in his temples, and throughout his entire body. His head throbbed, but the pain was only a distraction. He could hear the fear in her voice. The strain. She was trying to hold it together ... for him and the girls.

"Helen? You still there?"

After ten beats, he couldn't wait any longer. He glanced at the cell phone to see how the coverage was. It had been spotty lately, with complete outages alternating with seemingly interminable busy signals.

"I'm still here. It's just that ... I don't know, George. Everyone in the neighborhood has gone completely nuts."

There was another pause, and George let out a quiet hiss of breath between his teeth. He stared at the walls of his hotel room. It was new, built less than a year ago. He had spent a few weeks in it over the past few months and liked staying there. The sink wasn't rusty, and the wallpaper wasn't peeling like the dive in which he'd been forced to shack up on previous trips to

Gallatin.

"Do you remember the Patels?"

George shook off his reverie, the beige walls of his room fading into the background as he tried to think.

"No ... oh, wait! The Indian family that moved in down on Sycamore two years ago?"

"Yes. They were attacked last night! In their home! God, George, I don't know what happened, but Angela said it was a bunch of teenagers. A bunch of psychotic teenagers from around the neighborhood. She said that when the police got there, it was a mess. Mr. Patel was already dead, and his wife ... I don't even know if I can believe what she said happened to her."

"What about the kids?"

"Huh?"

George rubbed his temples. He was wound too tightly and was about to snap. Any time Helen told him about trouble when he was out of town, it was like this. Being helpless to do anything about it made him angry, and sooner or later he couldn't hide it from her. He took a deep breath and let it out slowly, counting backwards from ten.

"Their kids. What happened to their kids?"

"Oh. I don't know. Angela didn't say. God, I hope they're okay. But with all the crazies around here, I hate to imagine."

George nodded, even though Helen couldn't see it. He knew what she was talking about. The panic was palpable, thick in the air. The nutjobs weren't only in his neighborhood; they were everywhere. Running around on the streets spouting tales of doom or spreading chaos, using the approaching storm as an excuse to do horrible things. It was like the LA riots from the early nineties magnified a thousand times over.

Yesterday, when he had arrived in Gallatin, half the staff of the company he was working with was out sick. The Operations Manager had rolled his eyes as he told him about it. More likely they were playing hooky, using the worldwide mass hysteria as an excuse. His comment was, "Once this blows over, they'll be back, embarrassed they got so freaked out."

This morning, George awoke to the sounds of sirens and fire trucks, bullhorns and helicopters. The local news teams were going nuts, reporting on flash fires and random acts of violence, not only in the city, but in the suburbs as well. The National Guard had been called in, and they were working with the local authorities to restore peace. Rumors had it that the virus had touched down all over the region. There were unconfirmed reports of infections in Cincinnati and Dayton, as well as Columbus. The government would neither confirm nor deny any of it, simply saying that they were on high alert and everyone in the medical community, both domestically and internationally, was focused on finding a rapid cure.

"So how are you holding up?" He hated asking the question, knowing what the likely response would be.

"Helen?"

George could hear her breathing, so he knew they hadn't been disconnected.

"Helen, are you okay?" He was getting nervous. It was not just breathing he could hear; it was something else. The hairs stood up on the back of his neck. Helen was crying. She was trying to hold it back, but he could hear it over the hiss of the cellular connection.

"I'm scared, George."

The words were a whisper. They stopped George, froze his lips shut. Helen rarely cried and never said she was scared.

"I don't know what to do. You're not here, and Angela told me she and Hank are going to take the kids and head down to Lake Cumberland. Roxy and Deb are flipping out. It's all happening so fast, I feel like I'm losing my mind ..."

George was antsy about everything he had seen and heard in Gallatin since arriving ... and now his wife was telling him it was just as bad up in Wildwood. He'd called in to Raynor, the company with which he was contracted, at eight that morning, and there had been no answer. After three failed attempts to reach anyone, George left a message on the operations manager's voice mail, telling the man to call him on his cell. It was ten now, and there had been no call.

"Angela told me we could come with her-"

"NO!"

George was startled by his own vehement response. Angela

and Hank, their next-door neighbors, were good friends of the family. Their youngest daughter was Deb's age, so they had spent plenty of time together.

"Look, I ... I know things are screwed up right now. I know that! But I'll get back home, sweetie. I promise."

"But the roads are already being shut down, George! It's on the news. Time is running out. Hank knows a lot of back roads, and they have the camper. You could head down that way-"

"No, no, no. Please listen to me! It's dangerous out there. Way too dangerous for you to be bumming a ride with our neighbors. You know those lunatics attacking people in the neighborhood? Imagine what it's like out on highways. Even on the 'back roads' Hank knows. People are desperate, Helen. Desperate and dangerous."

The words spilled out of George's mouth at a rapid clip, and he was surprised at the level of derision in his voice when he mentioned Hank's name. The man was a friend, but all George could feel was anger and distrust toward him, as if his neighbor were trying to steal his family away.

A headache settled in behind his eyes as he tried to calm down. George was frightening himself with his words and couldn't imagine what they were doing to his wife. But he couldn't stop. He could feel his family slipping away.

"Don't go. I'm begging you, Helen. Please don't leave! I'll get back to you, I swear to God."

"Don't you dare blaspheme, George Montgomery. Not even now!"

George's tongue stuck to the roof of his mouth for a moment. The abrupt criticism was a sharp slap. It was a reprimand only his wife would use at a time like this. Before he knew it, a grin was creeping onto his face. That was Helen for you.

There was a pause in the conversation, as there always was after a stern reprimand. George knew Helen was composing herself, probably running her fingers through her fiery red hair. It was a habit she didn't realize she had. There would be a tilt of her head, then she would latch on to a few strands and run them between her fingers. Once she was done, it was as if all was right with the world again.

"So what do you suggest we do?"

George slumped back onto the hotel bed. His breathing felt less constricted, and the stiffness in his neck was loosening.

"Stay in the house—hear me out, please! I know everything is crazy around there, but it's no better anywhere else. The world is ... I don't know a better way to put it than that it's falling apart. I know you're scared. I'm sure the girls are too. I sure as hell know I am. So the last thing you need to be doing right now is wandering around trying to find some other place to hide when your best bet is to stay right where you are."

Helen was quiet once again, digesting what her husband had said.

"You only have to hole up until I get back home. Just a few days and we can figure out together what we should do. We'll take the Explorer and go wherever you want. Hopefully things will have settled down by then."

"I thought you said everything was falling apart."

"I did. I don't really know what to think right now. All I know is that it's dangerous out there, and there's only one place I know I can find you. Not in some cabin at Lake Cumberland, and not on some dirt road out in the sticks."

George heard his wife exhale. She still wasn't certain, but she knew that his position made sense.

"There's enough food and water to last you a month or more, not that I think it will come to that. There are some boards out in the garage ... now I know you won't like putting big holes in the walls, but just to be safe-"

"Okay! Okay! You don't have to keep pushing; you've convinced me, you big doofus."

George felt a zing of excitement rush through him.

"So you'll stay?"

"Yes! Yes already! I told you we would. What more do you want? For me to cross my heart and-"

"Don't say that."

George regretted the words as soon they were out of his mouth. He felt like slamming his fist into his forehead and cursing his stupidity as he gritted his teeth and closed his eyes.

"Okay. Yeah. Okay, I won't."

Helen's voice was subdued, the playfulness he had heard moments before gone.

"I love you."

"I love you too. You know I do. Forever and ever."

"Come back to us, George. Please. Get home. Be safe—don't do anything stupid, but get back to us as fast as you can."

"You know I will. I'm out of here in one hour. I should have never come here in the first place. You were right. It might take me a while, but you know it's not far. I might have to take one or two back roads myself, but I will make it back to you."

"Promise me, George. Promise us."

"I promise, Helen. You and the girls. Tell them Daddy will be home soon."

Two minutes later, they were still saying goodbye. George was afraid to lose the connection, because getting one again was iffy at best, but Helen had to go. She was already talking about how she and the girls were going to board up the doors and windows to the house. She had to tell Angela they would not be coming with them and say their goodbyes. Toward the end, Helen's voice sounded almost normal. She had an agenda, a purpose. Helen was not helpless; she was taking charge of the situation, which was when she was at her best.

As he hung up, George stepped over to the window, pushing the heavy drapery aside and peering down at the parking lot. He had no idea how many cars would normally be at the hotel on a weekday midmorning, but was certain it was typically more than the three he currently saw. There were muffled sounds coming from the street, from the opposite side of the building—more bullhorns and sirens. George tried to ignore them as he gazed at the green Explorer. It was parked in the spot next to the hotel exit.

He turned and moved over to the dresser, opening the drawers and pulling out the small amount of clothes he had in them, shoving them in the suitcase sitting on the end of the bed. As he packed, George whistled.

Five minutes later, just as he was about to leave, he heard a loud knocking at the door.

***

Now ... August 13th

George could hear the crickets outside the car. It was dark, the starlight casting a delicate glow that showed him the path he needed to take. He found a flashlight in the glove compartment—a gift from Ben that would come in handy. He covered the light with his hand as he flipped it on to make sure it worked. The red ring that formed on his palm confirmed that it did, and he switched the flashlight off.

He had been hiding in the park near his house for several hours, waiting for darkness to fall. After seeing what had happened in Willowsburg, he was relieved to see that his hometown of Wildwood hadn't burnt to the ground, even though it was full of the infected. His arrival had stirred up plenty of the stiffs, and he'd been forced to drive up and down a variety of residential streets for over an hour, in an effort to confuse as many of the ghouls as possible. When he was certain that most of them were clumped together behind the Corsica, he sped up and easily eluded their pursuit, leaving them confused and frustrated and, most importantly, out of his way.

He then drove toward his neighborhood and stopped at a small park a little over a block from his house. It appeared abandoned, the swing sets and picnic tables standing solitary sentinel against the madness of the outside world. George pulled off the grass and into a small stand of trees as he waited for the undead townsfolk he'd stirred up with his arrival to settle back down.

He could almost see his house from where he was parked. Being this close after all this time and not being able to return home immediately was agony. But George knew he needed the cover of night to hide his movements.

When it grew dark outside, he opened the car door, leaving the keys in the ignition. He shut it fast so the dome light wouldn't advertise his presence. Waiting, he listened for the sound of footsteps on the plush grass and heard none. He felt a prickle of fear, but did his best to brush it aside. His long journey was almost finished.

George looked out across the park toward the houses in the distance. He saw no movement in the starlit night. The infected were not the only creatures he feared. His neighborhood had been filled with plenty of pets. He figured most were dead, eaten by their ravenous masters, but was sure a few had escaped that fate and had gone feral, scrounging for food wherever they could find it. Images of wild packs of dogs floated through his mind.

George clenched his fists and shook his head. It was a stupid thing to worry about. No stray dog was going to keep him from his family. He would stay quiet and stick to the shadows. Nothing was going to stand in his way.

He moved in the direction of his house.

***

July 1st

"Honey, I don't know how long I have. I've been trying all day to get a hold of you. I doubt the connection will last very long."

"Oh George, thank God! Where are you? We got the boards up. We nailed the doors shut and covered all the ground floor windows. We should be safe now. When are you going to be home? We need you here. Now."

George rubbed his forehead and closed his eyes. Getting in touch with Helen was only a minor relief right now. He perched on his stiff cot and tried to blot out the noise of the other refugees in the gymnasium. He needed to focus on his wife.

"I ... I'm still in Gallatin, honey." He sped on before she could respond. "Listen to me. The National Guard took me out of my hotel about thirty minutes after we hung up yesterday. They didn't give me any choice. They wouldn't listen. They don't care that I have to get home. They were holding machine guns on us. They shoved us in a truck and brought us here. I was strip searched and tossed into a high school gym along with about four hundred other people, as best I can guess."

There was silence on the line. George moved his fingers down to his eyes, which ached from the nagging headache that would not go away. The gym had gotten too crowded, and they were still putting up more cots. His efforts to talk to the military personnel guarding them had met with discouraging results. The National Guardsmen inside the gym had no information and refused to let anyone speak to an officer above the rank of sergeant. All he could get out of them was that things would settle down in a day or two, and then they would be able to go home. For now, they said, it was best to just stay calm and relax. No one was allowed to leave the confines of the school—things outside were dangerous, but under control. Despite the reassurances of the young soldiers, the safeties were off on their weapons, and they were getting edgier by the minute.

"I WILL get home. I swear it. You know I will, Helen. Nothing will keep me here longer than absolutely necessary."

"You promised me, George. You promised our girls." There was a slight pause, a hesitation. "Things in the neighborhood ... they're bad. God, it's bad here."

Every word gashed George like a razor blade. His strong wife, the brave one who was afraid of no one and never backed down, was terrified.

"Helen. Listen to me." The connection was fuzzy, but holding up for the moment.

"I need you to believe me, Helen. I will get home. I swear on my life. No matter what it takes, I'm coming for you." George took a breath and looked around. There were hundreds of refugees packed in like sardines, and most looked as distraught as he did. A few people, bunched together as families, were making the most of it, like this was some sort of adventure, as they tried to keep their spirits up. Quite a few people were on cell phones having similar frantic conversations, while others were just trying to get a signal.

George had to get out of this place.

"Do you believe me?"

He waited, the seconds ticking away. He feared the connection was lost as he spoke again. "Helen?"

"I do."

George heard the words clearly. He loosened his grip on the phone and found that he could breathe again.

***

August 13th

George stood beside the old blue ash that had stood in the

Caldwells' yard for decades. It was a good thirty feet high with roots that he assumed ran beneath their entire lawn. As he brushed against its rough surface, he looked down the street. When his eyes rested on the front of his house, George's heart raced.

It looked okay. There was plenty of damage in the neighborhood, and a few of the houses looked gutted. Not due to fire—George had seen no indication of burning, although several power lines were down. Mostly it was just shattered glass and gaping holes where doors once stood. But his house was in good condition.

A few other houses looked fine despite the weeds and wild grass overrunning the lawns. There were still a few cars on the street and in driveways, though it looked like most of George's neighbors had abandoned ship early on.

He took one more look out onto the street. There wasn't any movement. With no weapon except the plastic flashlight, George's only option would be to run if he came across any trouble.

He steeled himself and shot across the street. He hit the Peraltas' yard and crouched next to the large hedge spanning the front of the home. He paused and listened, but heard nothing.

Working his way to the back of his neighbors' house, George was grateful there was no fence to contend with. That was why he had chosen their yard. He could get to his house with minimal hassle.

He moved closer to his home, maneuvering between his neighbors' bushes and trees. He stood behind their shed and looked into his back yard.

It was as he had left it. Memories gripped him as he scanned the small deck and French doors Helen had him install a couple of years ago. The windowpanes on the doors were intact, and it was far too dark to see if there was any plywood nailed in place behind them. The other windows on the ground level of the two-story house were all dark. The desire to turn on the flashlight and have a closer look was tempting, but George resisted the urge.

The house was tan, but in the dark it looked more like a drab off-white. Even from this closer vantage point, the property still appeared to be in decent shape. George knew that was a good sign. There appeared to be no points of forced entry. He looked at the upstairs window and saw that the curtains were drawn.

"Daddy's come home. I kept my promise."

He could barely hear his own whispered words as he gazed up at the bedroom windows. The girls were probably up there. George could feel them inside the house. As he got closer, he was certain of it.

His eyes moved back to the deck and then below it. There it was: the window well. There were three total, with the other two on the sides of the house. This one was the easiest to reach without exposing himself to the street. They had taped black garbage bags over them years ago, and he knew Helen wouldn't have bothered boarding them up. They were sunk halfway into the ground, and it was going to be difficult enough for someone limber to climb through, let alone one of the stiffs wandering the street.

As he crossed the yard and drew close to the window well, he gave one last look up at the second floor.

"Soon, babe. I'll be with you real soon."

***

July 1ˢᵗ

"I think some of our neighbors have been infected."

George shook his head in disbelief. "Are you sure? I mean, there are a lot of people going nuts. Maybe it just looked like they had the virus because they'd gone around the bend. It wouldn't surprise me with some of the yahoos living in our neighborhood."

"No, George. It's not just a few people flipping out. Rob Kerr got mauled in his own front yard. Just as he was leaving with Kendra and the kids. It was awful."

"Honey, people talk," George protested. "They like to make up garbage. What? Did Angela tell you that? Rob probably got attacked by someone-"

"No! George, listen to me. I saw it with my own eyes. It was horrible! They were biting on him, and he was screaming. Kendra was beating them with a broom handle, and they just ignored her. There was blood everywhere. God ... the blood."

George's confidence wavered, but he refused to be sucked in by the panic gripping his wife. "Well, did someone help them? I mean as these lunatics started chewing on Rob was there anyone trying to stop it?"

"Yes! Of course there was! Several of the neighbors who were outside came over to help."

"And?"

"And what?"

George silently counted down from ten. "And then what happened to Rob?"

"I don't know. I couldn't ... I couldn't watch anymore." Helen stopped, and George knew she was trying to collect herself. "It was absolutely horrible! That anyone could do such a thing."

"Do you know who it was who attacked him?"

"How should I know? They were smeared in blood and ... Good Lord; there was so much blood ..."

"Okay, okay." George placated her, knowing the conversation was going nowhere. He switched gears.

"The house is set, right?"

"Yes. I told you we took care of everything."

"I know, but I want to make sure my girls are all safe until I can get out of this stink hole and get back home."

"Speaking of your girls, one of them wants to talk to you."

"Okay, put her on."

George took a deep breath and tried to smile. His daughter would not see it, but it would help him maintain the pretense of being in good spirits. He was expecting Roxanne, the twelve year old, so he was surprised when he heard the bright and cheery voice of Deb, his younger daughter.

"Hi, Daddy!"

"Hey, baby! How are you guys doing?"

"We're okay. Roxy's ... we're all okay."

There was a pause. George was worried that at any moment the connection might go dead, and he wanted to squeeze in as much conversation as he could before it did.

"Daddy's going to be home real soon, all right?"

"I know." There was another pause filled with hissing and crackling as their tenuous connection wavered in and out. George didn't speak, wondering if it was sadness he heard in his daughter's voice or just the faulty connection.

"Daddy? When you get home, can we play Battleship again? I know I can beat you this time."

George smiled. Of course Deb wanted to play a game with him. She was the competitive one in the family. Whether it was basketball, soccer, or just a board game, Deb's dream was to beat her old man. She had a sharp mind and was naturally athletic, just like George. He knew it was only a matter of time before she was able to whip him at anything she tried her hand at.

"You bet, honey. I promise."

"Good."

As George envisioned the smile on his daughter's face, his own grew.

"I love you, Daddy. Get home soon, okay?"

A sudden rush of emotion choked him for a moment. George fought back the tears as he tried to respond. Before he could, he realized that Deb was already gone.

Before Helen got back on, he whispered a response to his daughter's plea.

"Daddy will be home real soon, sweetie."

***

August 13th

The glass spiderwebbed, and a few shards tinkled into the basement. George tensed at the noise. The plastic flashlight had survived smashing the glass, but the noise had been louder than he expected. George turned so his feet faced the window and tried to delicately push the cracked pane of glass out of the frame. After a few seconds, most of it, except for a few small slivers, tumbled into the basement.

The black plastic sheeting that had covered the window now floated loosely about the opening. George listened carefully, wondering if the sound of broken glass might alert his family. When he heard nothing, he guessed they were on the top floor.

There was no chance they would have heard something all the way down in the basement.

George plucked away the few remaining bits of glass on the bottom of the frame and poked his head inside. A small amount of starlight snuck past his broad shoulders, but he couldn't see anything. He turned around and slid his legs through the window. As they dangled above the floor, he stopped and listened to the outside world one last time. There was no indication that his assault on the window had drawn any attention, so he carefully slid into the basement. He held his breath for a moment and waited. Still nothing. Moving fast, he pushed the tattered black plastic sheet over the hole he had made.

Heart racing, George flipped on the flashlight and maneuvered through his basement toward the stairs.

*

The decrepit creature had lived five doors down from George before she was bitten. In the past month, she had moved little, except when attacking a few of the neighbors in a nearby house. After that, the only thing there was to eat was a cat and the litter of kittens to which it had just given birth. The feline had been hiding out under a bush in the yard next to George's house. After the ghoul fed, there had been little else to attract her attention, so she sat there, motionless, for several weeks.

Until she heard George breaking the glass to his basement window.

It was muffled, barely audible, and yet nearby. Her shriveled throat rattled as the pathetic wretch moved her jaws open and shut. A thick, oily substance lubricated her mouth. Soon, her desiccated tongue scraped at her lips as she moved closer to George's house.

The foul monster saw no one, but there was a scent on the air. The smell of sweat and pheromones. Her eyes widened as she crossed to the door at the side of the house and moaned with excitement.

*

George didn't hear the call of the infected outside as he crossed the basement to the staircase. He stirred up a layer of dust and pulled his shirt over his nose, worried he would start coughing.

As he set his foot on the first step, he envisioned Helen and the girls, surprised and overjoyed to see him. His heart was nearly bursting in anticipation.

As he reached the top of the steps, he heard the noise. At first it was barely noticeable. Just a faint tapping. It could have been anything: boards creaking, the house settling ... But George knew what it meant as he touched the doorknob, even before he heard the glass breaking at the side door.

He opened the door, the flashlight shining out onto his kitchen. He barely glanced at the piled pots and pans in the sink and the old appliances Helen had been nagging him to replace as he heard the moans coming from outside.

He sped through the kitchen. A brief glance at the door reassured him they were safe for the moment. There were a couple of thick two by fours nailed across the door over a piece of plywood. George could hear the hungry sounds of anticipation from outside and ignored them. There was probably only one of those things out there, but soon there would be others.

"Helen?"

The time for stealth was over. George rocketed through the family room toward the stairs leading to the second floor. He didn't want to frighten his girls. The noises coming from outside would be upsetting, but the sound of his voice would reassure them everything was okay.

"Roxy! Deb! It's me! Daddy's home! I finally made it!"

He didn't have much time. He had to get to his girls before the kitchen door shattered and a rush of stiffening bodies tumbled in.

As he reached the bottom of the steps, George hesitated, listening. Over the din from outside, there was another noise. Something trickling down from up above. The flashlight fell out of his boneless fingers, and George leaned forward, his hand gripping the banister. He held on tight, his legs weak beneath him.

His heart thundered as he heard the footsteps from up above, and George began to weep. He wiped the wetness from his eyes and tried to speak.

"I made it, baby. I finally made it home. I told you ... I promised you. Nothing was going to stop me from making it back to you and the girls."

George climbed the steps to his family.

***

July 1ˢᵗ

"So how are you going to get out of there?"

George tried to hold on to the residue of warm feelings the conversation with his daughter had given him.

"I'll figure something out. They won't be able to keep me here for long. This place isn't some kind of fortress; it's a damn high school gym."

"Don't curse, George." The words rolled off of Helen's tongue robotically, without thought. George's tried to think of a sharp rebuttal, but his weary mind refused to cooperate.

"Whatever you do, don't try anything foolish. I would rather you stay there for a day or two instead of getting shot."

"I won't do anything foolish, and you know it. Nothing that's going to get me killed."

George's ears turned beet red. He knew he sounded like a petulant child.

"I know. I know, my darling. I just want you to be safe and come home in one piece. We just need you here really bad, George."

George tried to speak again, but hesitated, thinking about Helen's words.

"Is everything okay?"

After a few uncomfortable moments of waiting for a response, he knew. Something was wrong.

"Helen?"

"No, George. It's all right. Everything is fine. Nothing to worry about. I just miss you, and so do the girls. We need you so we can figure out where to go from here. If we should just leave town or ..."

The static was getting worse. The signal was fading, and they might have only a few moments left. George could sense that his wife was keeping something from him.

"Helen, please. Just tell me what it is. Quickly. Before I lose you."

The double meaning of the words was not lost on George as he shifted uncomfortably on his cot.

"Oh, it's nothing. No big deal."

He waited. Helen's words were a delicate lie she was weaving to lessen the blow. It was only making it worse.

"It's ... it's Roxy, George. She's not feeling well. She has a fever." He heard her exhale. "I have her in bed with a cold compress on her head. She took a hot bath, and I made her some soup. I'm sure she'll be fine."

George's mind raced. His daughter was sick in bed. It was no big deal; it had happened before. His girls always bounced back rapidly from any minor ailments they picked up.

Still, he did not feel right.

"When did she start feeling sick, hon?"

"I'm not exactly sure." Helen's tone was evasive. "Look, it really doesn't matter. She'll be okay in another day. As right as rain. I'm taking good care of her."

George's headache intensified, spurred by the sizzle and crack of the weak cell connection.

"HELEN!"

Several people near his cot turned to look at George, but every ounce of his attention was focused on the person at the other end of the phone line.

"Please, just tell me. If there's anything else, I have to know. Before I lose the connection! Please ..."

There was more silence on the other end, and every second he waited felt like an eternity.

"Really ... it's nothing. I swear, George. Nothing. It's just that, well ... before we boarded everything up, Angela and Hank came over one last time to try to convince me to go with them. I told them we were staying to wait for you. They argued with me. I never thought I would get into a fight with Angela, but we did. She told me I was stupid and that we were all going to die if we stayed here.

"George, I have never seen Angela so scared in all my life. She was screaming at me, pleading for me to go with them. Well, I lost it on her. I feel bad for doing it, but I couldn't help myself. Roxy and Deb were standing there, and she was scaring the daylights out of them. I started screaming back at her! George, I think we would have come to blows if Hank hadn't stepped in. He told Angela to back off, that they couldn't force us to go if we wanted to stay. George, he literally picked her up and carried her out of our house. It was crazy ..."

George waited. He knew it would be pointless to ask his wife to speed the story along to its conclusion, so he ground his teeth and listened to the rhythmic pounding of blood flowing through his ears.

"We went out on the porch to watch them go back to their house. They were already packed and ready to go. I told the girls to go inside, but of course they didn't listen. Angela was still screaming, and Hank was trying to put her in their truck. The camper was hooked up, and I think their kids had to be in the back because I didn't see them ... thank God they didn't see what happened."

George clenched his teeth tighter and squeezed the phone. He could feel it cutting into his palm.

"George, I ... oh, God George, it was awful!"

"It's okay. Take it easy, hon. Just tell me. You can do it."

"I don't know where he came from. He was just there, next to them. Maybe from between the houses or from behind the camper. I don't know. But he attacked Hank."

"Who, Helen? Who attacked Hank?"

"I don't know! Just some man! Some ragged, filthy man. He was covered in dirt and ... blood. My God, I think it was blood. That's all I know." George could hear the pain in Helen's voice. He wanted to tell her she could stop, she didn't have to keep speaking, but he couldn't.

"Hank dropped Angela on the ground and wrestled with the man. I ran over ... I don't know what I was thinking, as if I could do anything to help. But, George, the screams! Hank was screaming like I have never heard before!"

"I was getting closer as Angela got up. She was screaming along with Hank, and then I saw it. The man had bitten Hank!"

And he was still biting him, chewing on his arm like some pit bull. It was terrible."

George could feel his stomach churning. He had waited long enough, had been incredibly patient. He took a breath and held it in for a moment.

"Honey. Please. Just tell me what happened to Roxy."

Helen paused again.

"She tried to help them. I tried to stop her, George. I really did. But she grabbed her tennis racket. You remember the one she got for Christmas? She started beating on the man. I grabbed at her, but she had gone crazy."

George tried to breathe. It wasn't hard to believe Roxy would be the one to grab the most convenient weapon available and begin beating on some psychopath who had just attacked their neighbor. The girl knew no fear.

"What happened, Helen?"

George was losing his grip on reality. The gym and all the people inside it swam before his eyes. Helen was trying to tell him every last detail when all he wanted to know was what had happened to his daughter.

"Hank was able to pull the man off his arm. He was beating on him with everything he had. So was Angela. It was hard to see ..."

"WHAT THE HELL HAPPENED TO MY DAUGHTER?"

"It's nothing, George. Really. Just a little tiny scratch on her wrist. Hank pulled the man away, and she was fine. It barely broke the skin."

***

August 13th

"I made it, baby. I finally made it home. I told you ... I promised you. Nothing was going to stop me from making it back to you and the girls."

The stairs creaked beneath George's feet. He looked up, breathless and excited. There were shadows coming down the hall.

The noises outside were growing. Other ghouls had joined the first, its moans alerting them. They were at the door, and soon they would break it down to get inside.

"How is Roxy, baby? Is she okay? Are you and Deb okay? I missed you all so much."

George reached the top of the stairs, and as he looked across the landing, he saw his wife walking toward him. His two girls were trailing behind her.

He smiled and opened his arms. Their arms were thrown wide as well, ready to embrace him. There were ugly welts on Roxy's arms and legs where she had been tied up. The gag they had shoved in her mouth hung loosely around her neck, stained black in the slivers of moonlight that trickled through the windows. There were bite marks on Helen and Deb's arms and necks, but George didn't notice them. He didn't see the tint of corruption on their skin or smell the decay surrounding them. All he could see was his family: the three reasons he had fought to stay alive for as long as it had taken to get back to them, just as he had promised.

George felt a profound comfort as his beautiful red-haired wife fell into his arms. His daughters enclosed him in their embrace as well, and he closed his eyes, at peace.

"I'm home. I'm finally home."

*

Ten minutes later, the banging on the kitchen door slowed and then stopped altogether. Confused, the first ghoul that had come to the door sniffed the air and stood there, baffled. The others bounced off of her as they left, fading back into the shadows of George's yard. His neighbor raised her arm and scratched sadly at the door one last time. A few minutes later, she also turned to walk away. There was no longer anything inside the house that she wanted.

About the Author

Patrick D'Orazio resides in southwestern Ohio with his wife, Michele, two children, Alexandra and Zachary, and two spastic dogs. A lifelong writer, he only recently decided that attempting to get published might be a better idea than continuing to toss all those stories he's been scribbling down over the years into a filing cabinet, never to be seen again.

Over twenty of his short stories appear or will be appearing in various anthologies from a wide array of different small press publishers. He has dipped his toes into a variety of genres, including horror, science fiction, fantasy, erotica, Bizarro, western, action-adventure, apocalyptic, and comedy.

Beyond the Dark is the final book in the Dark Trilogy. It is preceded by the novels *Comes the Dark* and *Into the Dark*, both of which are also available through the Library of the Living Dead Press.

You can see what Patrick is up to via his website at www.patrickdorazio.com or over at the forums at www.thelibraryofthelivingdead.com.

CPSIA information can be obtained at www.ICGtesting.com
Printed in the USA
LVOW071942010212

266575LV00018B/61/P